Frances Hubbard Turnbull

Val-Maria

A romance of the time of Napoleon I

Frances Hubbard Turnbull

Val-Maria
A romance of the time of Napoleon I

ISBN/EAN: 9783337350529

Printed in Europe, USA, Canada, Australia, Japan

Cover: Foto ©Andreas Hilbeck / pixelio.de

More available books at **www.hansebooks.com**

DAL-MARIA. ❧ ❧
A ROMANCE OF THE
TIME OF NAPOLEON I.
BY MRS. LAWRENCE TURNBULL,
AUTHOR OF THE CATHOLIC MAN.

"A LITTLE CHILD SHALL LEAD THEM."

PHILADELPHIA :

J. B. LIPPINCOTT COMPANY.

1893.

Printed by J. B. Lippincott Company, Philadelphia.

MOST

TENDERLY INSCRIBED

TO

A LITTLE CHILD

WHO HAS ATTAINED TO THE FULNESS OF
LIFE AND LOVE.

CHAPTER FIRST.

VER the edge of the lawn, as far as the eye could reach, one of the windings of the river that crossed and recrossed the estate of Val-Maria was spanned by a bridge of stone wrought with rude carving, after the fashion of the days in which the château had been built; one of the piers on the farther side had been finished as a shrine, rising into a column above the railing of the bridge, upon which, under a Gothic canopy somewhat unevenly corroded by the touch of time, was an image of the tutelary saint of Val-Maria, statue and shrine alike pre-

3

senting but the most primitive conception or realization of art; neither had conception nor realization gained in beauty, as some rude art-creations do, from that mellowing touch which had stained its surfaces and obliterated its outlines. But the faithful, who still came occasionally with votive offerings and whispered requests, were the freer to find on this Virgin's face whatever expression it was in their hearts to give her, while with her lack of beauty these simple village-folk were not concerned.

This bridge divided the quarters of the dependants of the château, as distinguished from the house-servants, from the château itself; for the one street of the modest village started directly from the small square on which the bridge fronted, and the low stone cottages, tiled and moss-softened, which lined one side of the unshaded street, began on the square, with the cottage of the laundress, which was precisely like the others, save for its great advantage of being nearer the willows that grew on the river's bank, to whose great roots a little space had been graciously granted before the uncompromising pavement of the square began. Under these trees the laundress kept her benches, with the tubs, where she and her mother before her had been seen whitening the fine linen of the château; so impressed was she with the dignity of her office that she would gladly have brought up her little daughter to the same post of honor, but that the times were filled with a great unrest, whose echo—of the scantest and faintest, still an unsettling echo—had penetrated even to that short, sun-flooded, cobble-paved street.

It was not always talk of the doings at the great house, nor even of the threadbare village gossip, when the baker, in his white cap and apron, having delivered his daily quota of rolls to the grand liveried servant from the château, and having duly measured off his *pain-du-pays* in the required lengths to his village customers, passed under his low door-way— decorated, by way of sign, with the black and gold card announcing his baker's license—for the mid-day lounge under the willows, which was his custom in fine weather. With discretion, too, he left his door ajar, displaying his few remaining metres of bread ranged against the wall, and reaching from floor to ceiling, that his thrifty neighbors might see how far the day's baking had gone beyond its needs, and avail themselves of the few centimes of reduction at evening sale, to make their family provision for the following day; thus should he calculate more exactly how large a sponge to provide at the evening's mixing—for every village-mouth and its average capacity was estimated by each baker who had held the post, and who put his mind in his work—and thus it happened, not unfrequently, that the baker's family also had eaten luxuriously of bread of the day's baking, without transgressing that provincial instinct which held extravagance in horror.

Now, as he settled himself comfortably with his pipe under the willows, it was frequently with a part of the Paris *Journal* from the great house, as a text for his simple comments, delivered sermon-wise, to his unwilling auditor, his sister, who had been wont to sing at her work as the suds foamed up over her bare arms, and overflowed into the crevices of the round cobbles below, with rich possibilities of moss. She had been taught that life was good in Val-Maria; the children had always enough to eat, and new sabots when the old ones were outgrown; and the countess was pleased with her work, and there was not too much to do; and when they were sick, the countess came herself; and once, when little Jean had died, she had sent a grand physician from the château, who came from Paris for Monsieur Felix, and she had thought the Virgin of Val-Maria was very kind to them! But Pierre said it was not so; he said any man could be a soldier, and soldiers could be generals, and the generals were the nobles nowadays, and the nobles had the power— the people gave them the power. And if it wasn't for the musket—for he was stronger in his arms than in his shoulders and his legs, from kneading so much bread—why, he'd rather deal with blood than flour, and leave a title to little Nanette—who knows?

Then for Pierre would follow a period of tranquil dreaming over the sweetness of a title for little Nanette, or at least some glory for himself, under the great Napoleon; while his sister absently rubbed holes in the fine damask of the château, as she wondered what it all meant, and why Pierre was sometimes so bitter against the sweet lady at the château; and Monsieur le Comte—Pierre said he had no right to be a count—he hadn't won by fighting, and if his father was there, and his father's father before him, it was no reason at all, Pierre said, but all the more, he had had it long enough.

But when the neat-capped Jeanne came out of her cottage to call Pierre to his soup, he stopped his grumbling without an effort, and helped his sister in with her long board piled high with snowy linen twists, contentedly enough, and whistled over his bread when he was kneading, just as he used to do—that day and many days thereafter—and no more talk of battles and titles until the fit came upon him again, with some new grand doings in Paris, of which accounts had sifted to Val-Maria. And this time, perchance, it would be a new tune. "Everything fine was in Paris —there was no life in living away from its fêtes! Napoleon kept everything stirring—*he* was a man! He could turn the world round his finger! And here in Val-Maria!"

And Yvonne, who had interposed with a timid, "Come then, Pierre, we have still our Madonna Val-Maria; thou should'st burn a candle to her, if all goes so badly," would be met with a shrug of the shoulders, and perhaps a silence, or words not more comforting.

"Ah, well then, I forget; thou sayest true; we have still our Madonna Val-Maria. In Paris, *va*, it is not of the Madonna Val-Maria that one occupies oneself; but of the 'Little Corporal!' Thou, then, find me the candles, and I will burn them!"

And again Pierre returned to knead his bread, often with the snatch of an army song; while Yvonne, not understanding

Pierre's restless words, but wholly contented with her own lot, was yet sad at heart, and sometimes dropped a tear on the polished bit that was still hot from her iron.

And when the day was done she would raise one of the children in her arms to offer a flower to the Madonna Val-Maria, and to ask her to be always good to them and to the sweet lady of the château.

CHAPTER SECOND.

"*ADONNA Mia!*" said the boy, caressingly, "tell me about our Consul; oh, I *want* to see him!"

The musical tones took on a sudden eagerness as the boy clasped his hands about his mother's neck and laid his beautiful head for an instant upon her shoulder, pressing his glowing cheek to hers. But before she could answer him, he unwound his arms and bounded across the velvet lawn to gather a rose that had caught his restless glance in the very moment of his caress, but it was only another tribute of the adoring love with which Felix ceaselessly worshipped the pale, beautiful mother whose life was devoted to him. Presently he was beside her again, opening a jewelled clasp in her dress to fasten his bud, using the freedom of one who knows himself so tenderly beloved that he can do nothing amiss: and she watched him, smiling silently down on his loving homage, while the eager fingers rearranged the folds he had disturbed in introducing his flower.

Oh, Love, artist beyond all others, creating the highest beauty, and imparting the power to receive its fullest and holiest impression, how is it possible to convey in words the feelings with which this mother clasped her treasure; her exquisite realization of the gift, in the nearness of the child-heart to her own, almost triumphing for the moment over the dumb, hopeless agony which held her ceaselessly in thrall, beneath the outward sunshine of a home that seemed too near to heaven to know the touch of pain !

"My rose is like the sunset!" he cried, joyously, as he threw himself down on the lawn beside her, and laid his head on her knee. "It is so beautiful up there in the clouds; *everything* is so beautiful. Now tell me, *Madre mia,*" the childish voice rang out, eagerly.

"What is it you want to know, my darling?"

"Oh, everything, for our Consul is such a wonderful man! Monsieur l'Abbé likes me to know about noble men. Is his face beautiful too? I should like his face to be beautiful, so all the people would love him."

A slight shadow crossed the mother's face and her hand strayed soothingly through the rich hair tossed back on her lap, which seemed almost to make a radiance about the head of the boy, as he lay there looking up into the sky: he was like a bird, full of eager twittering motions which came from the exuberance of his nature, yet he was almost an artist in his passionate, unchildlike appreciation of beauty, and the changes in the glowing evening clouds reflected themselves in answering moods and varying lights upon the upturned mobile face. He grew quieter under the caressing touch, lying almost still, which was

2

rare for him.   He was absorbed in delight and he forgot to repeat his question.

" Do you remember the little bust that stood on papa's study-table before we came home?" (the great house in Paris was never "home" to them ; all the dearer associations had clustered about this estate of Val-Maria to which the count had brought his bride very early in their married life : here little Felix was born, and here had been granted days so filled with joy that if no more such golden hours were to follow them, it would still be possible to live through long years upon their memory; and in this thought the young countess had grown more beautiful, year by year, with a nun-like beauty, as she became paler, while the deepening shadows about her eyes and mouth changed to a smile of ineffable tenderness at the mere sight of her husband or her child).   The luminous eyes fixed full upon her recalled her to a sense of needed effort— it was so easy to drift into a yearning revery of the time before she knew the truth !   She stooped and kissed the child passionately.   "I forget how little you were when I took you to Paris; you could not remember the bust. I must have it brought for your very own. You shall see that it is a beautiful head, my Felix."

"Oh, dear mamma! I know it must be beautiful," the boy cried, springing to his feet. "But what is it like? I cannot wait to know!"

"One must wait sometimes," the mother said, smiling at his impatience. "Sometimes, my Felix, it is strong and beautiful to wait."

"To wait means to grow strong in patience," said Monsieur l'Abbé, when the boy told him of his mother's gift, repeating her words almost as she had spoken them. "And to be strong in patience makes men noble."

It was pathetic to see how the mother and teacher strove together to store the fullest sweetness against life's time of stress for their beautiful Felix.

"It makes men noble and beautiful," Felix assented, coming close to his tutor with exuberant, springing motions, and emphasizing with his whole graceful little figure the two chief words. "Is our Consul like that? Is he strong and noble?"

"Madame la Comtesse will order the bust at once; I must hasten to make this waiting short," the kind abbé responded with a smiling evasion of the eager question.

There had been a memorable day in the lives of Montal and his wife of which they never spoke, though often as they paced the lawn together, with the child flitting from flower to flower before them, its memory tightened his hand-clasp on the fragile fingers resting on his arm—for they were lovers yet. It was the day when the count had first felt sure that she was breaking her heart in silence over the sorrow he had tried to keep from her. "We must bear all things together," he had said, putting his strong arm around her and turning up her face to his; "we have no separate life."

Her eyes were swimming in tears, through which she could not force the quivering smile that had never before failed her, and she needed his silent comforting, before she could say brokenly, "It is about Felix : let me *not* tell you, Louis—it will be too hard for you."

"My wife is first," he answered, vainly trying to command his voice. "And Felix——"

They bowed their heads and fell into each other's arms: the cross seemed too heavy for them to bear. God only knows, as He alone gives the strength, how one may rise from such unutterable agony and take up the common life again, and seem to live above the shadow.

It was Louis who broke the long silence; his words were very low and calm. "It is God's will. Dear, shall we cloud the little life of our darling by our grief—I think he is troubled sometimes at your sadness—or, shall we rouse ourselves and make it the happiest life that ever gladdened our earth?"

She assented with a wan smile.

Her husband watched her with troubled eyes. He would have given his own for the life of the child, but he had wrestled with his agony until submission had come. She was awed by the expression of his face as he bent

b　　　2*

over her—pale, set, inexpressibly tender—for she recognized suddenly that it was strengthened and spiritualized by the consecration of this accepted sorrow.

She clung to him, convulsed with pity. "Oh, Louis, how long have you known it?"

"Always, my darling; they told me at his birth." The words came very slowly, but his tones and motions quieted her.

"And you have never had one happy hour with our boy! My poor Louis!'

He could only soothe her silently, as she lay like a crushed flower in his arms.

"It is only that we *know*," he said, at length, "and it may not be for years, they say. To others these separations come often without warning. We will fill his life with gladness, my darling—it shall be your mission—and, together, God shall make us strong to miss no gladness while Felix is left us."

Perhaps no other words could have held such strength for her; she felt the greatness of a struggle which could thus have conquered, and she must be brave to comfort him : how precious, too, should be the days that were already numbered! their grief must not be the undoing of all the joy of the beautiful childish presence ; and she, too, lifted her cross with consecrated hands.

As she looked up and tried to smile, her pale face flushed with a sudden resolve. "Since he is never to be a man," she said, bravely, "since he will not have to battle with life, and he has everything that love can give—I can only think of this to make him happier—do you think it would be right, Louis, to keep all knowledge of evil from him?"

"It is like the mother of our Felix," he answered, with all his heart in his eyes, triumphing over his pain: and more slowly—for the simple words were burdened with the meaning of their heavy cross—"For *our* little child, I think it would be right."

From that hour they never again named their trial to each other, only when some recognition of it became necessary in planning for their darling's welfare, they would look into each other's faces and gather strength for

their promise to keep the sunshine very bright
on the pathway of little Felix.

They had scarcely controlled their emotion
when the boy came bounding towards them,
over the orange-terrace upon which the long
windows opened, with his arms full of flowers
for " Madre mia!"

" Why is my beautiful mamma so sorry?"
he cried, pressing up against her with tender
sympathy. " Papa will bring you out into the
sunshine: it is so beautiful out there, you
can't be sorry any more. And I have made
your garden-chair so pretty for you to sit in!"

And so she went with her two lovers—
her Christian knight and their beautiful boy—
over the broad stone terrace with its great tubs
of royal pottery, filled with orange-trees, fra-
grant with perfume and beautiful with their
red-gold fruit, down the steps of other terraces, gravelled, marble-bordered, and set with
oleanders and cacti and palms, all in their
royal vases, a decoration as costly as the statues
that gleamed among them. And still another,
box-trimmed, in quaint fantasies, where prim,

old-fashioned garden-flowers grew in their own beds of carefully-kept earth, led to a stiff alley of giant poplars, in which were scattered stone seats made of thick slabs, resting on elaborately carved supports, grotesque and black with time. And still beyond, out on the smooth lawn, where all the sky was clear and bright above them, stood the rustic modern chair which the little artist's hands had interlaced with morning-glories.

As the mother sat on her throne of love, made beautiful by that fragile, passing bloom, the sunlight flooded the upturned faces of the group—that perfect, mysterious group of three —with a glory like a halo, and though her heart was breaking, she tried not "to be sorry any more."

CHAPTER THIRD.

EANWHILE the child had grown in knowledge and in beauty day by day, and still more in that undefinable charm which is independent of either, but more potent than both, a winsomeness and grace which drew all hearts to him. His joyousness was infectious; his power of loving combined the perfect confidence of childhood with the fervor of a maturer nature; and his passionate, unchildlike appreciation of beauty proved the depth of the poet-artist soul that illumined his face and modulated his voice so exquisitely that one who had ever heard its tones could not forget them.

This love of beauty had come down to him through generations, nourished and quickened by the art-treasures which filled the old Florentine palace in which his mother had passed her girlhood; and knowing well the strength of this passion for beauty, by it his wise and tender watchers guided the boy into a rare knowledge of the thoughts and motives that make life noble. And very beautiful it was to see the young soul growing fair and strong in the sunlight of their loving ministrations, and knight-like through his stanch, unswerving fealty to truth—a noble legacy that had come to him direct from the English side of his father's house.

The boyhood of Louis, Comte de Montal, the father of little Felix, had been passed in the gracious Christian home of his grandfather on his mother's side, where, in an atmosphere that was vocal with the best thought of the best minds, in which neither heart nor head has been forgotten, the old man and the boy lived in close and loving companionship, the scholar renewing his youth as he saw his grandchild rapidly advancing in his own quaint admirations. So rapid, indeed, had this progress been, that when, at the age of fourteen, Louis lost this cherished companion and mentor, and returned to his home in France, to receive the education of a young French nobleman of those days, he had already acquired a love of knowledge, a fund of information, an acquaintance with the choicest biographies and the utterances of great men, that was unusual at a much riper age, together with a remarkable power of memorizing. With this habit, his early teachings had been, so to speak, woven into the boy's character; he could forget nothing that had been wrought for him with so much love; the books he had studied became his living friends, their teachings were vivified with his grandfather's voice, and the education of these early days laid the strong substructure of English simplicity and Christian truth upon which all that was added in later years, of grace or wisdom or courtliness, grew the more roundly, until Louis de Montal was known as one of the most Christian, enlightened, and devoted statesmen of his time.

From his mother Felix inherited his wondrous beauty and his passionate artistic temperament, the fervor of which had been tempered and vivified with the joyousness of his French ancestral blood, until the shadows that brooded over the darker faces of his Italian ancestry were sought in vain on the child's pure brow, and in the glorious eyes whose sternest moods showed only a sweet seriousness, intensifying at rare moments, with a spiritual meaning that seemed almost unearthly.

This intense love of beauty had its inconveniences at times. Felix was scarcely more than a baby when he first made acquaintance with the Madonna Val-Maria—quite too little to comprehend the importance of its position in the quaint village community—and Yvonne crossed herself even now, whenever she recalled the scene—the little one lifted high in the arms of Lucie the bonne, to reach the shrine with his dimpled, flower-filled hands, and lay his offering of roses at the Virgin's feet. Yvonne had left her linen and come forward with eager interest, for in her gentle soul she loved the child of the sweet lady at the château, and she wished that the Madonna might keep him from all harm.

"Come, then, Monsieur Felix, my angel! A little kiss with the rosy mouth for the good Madonna; it shall be like a prayer for thee!"

But Felix had dropped his flowers and was struggling downward with all the force of his baby strength. "No, no!" he protested, with the uncompromising frankness of his three years; "she is not a beautiful lady like my mamma! She is ugly—ugly; and she hasn't any face at all. I will not come to see her any more."

"*De grâce*, Monsieur Felix!" the nurse expostulated, as she smoothed out the multiform creases made in her fine embroidered apron by the little struggling feet; while Felix, set free, ran eagerly across the bridge to the spot where his mother stood waiting to receive his confidence of disappointment, reiterating as he clasped her close with his little loving arms, "She is so ugly—so ugly, *Madre mia!* I do not love her; why can't my papa get a beautiful one for me to love?"

"See, Felix, you have made poor Yvonne so sorry!" his mother answered, gently, pointing back to the shrine where the peasant knelt telling her rosary. "It is not beautiful to make any one sorry! We will go back, and my little one can pick up the flowers for Yvonne to give to the Madonna; perhaps that will make her glad. And then you shall come with me to the chapel and see the beautiful Saint Elizabeth, and mamma will tell you about the Madonna Val-Maria. When you are older, darling, you will know that love makes many things seem beautiful!"

In connection with the name of the estate there was a tradition to the effect that the first Count of Montal had made a pilgrimage to Rome to obtain the Papal benediction upon the château about to be erected, and that he had brought back with him, as a sign of favor, and specially blessed as a protectress of the peasantry, this Madonna, for whom the rude shrine had been constructed before one stone had been laid for the walls of the château— as a token, said the legend, that the counts of Montal should ever hold first the welfare of their people. The story, like the time-worn Madonna, was a relic of old feudal days, but its meaning flowed deep in the veins of the counts of Montal, making them gentle and considerate masters; and in later days, when feudalism was abolished, inclining them, aristocrats though they were, to a partial advocacy of radicalism—so far as the rights of the people were concerned; while the peasants, on their part, largely ascribed the favorable conditions of their life to the beneficent influence of the tutelary Saint of Val-Maria. Nor were they altogether wrong, since it was, indeed, to the teachings of the legend that they owed the valorous attitude of these true knights of Montal.

Something of this, as a reason for Yvonne's feeling for the Madonna Val-Maria, the countess tried in simple words to convey to little

Felix, but she was doubtful whether the child understood her, in spite of the intentness of his gaze while he listened to her story.

But the little fellow went back obediently, and gravely picking up the scattered flowers he laid them silently in Yvonne's hands, standing quite still beside her, and watching her curiously as she placed them at the foot of the shrine ; but when she turned towards him he fled hastily back to his mother's side, as if for protection from further demands of homage, and seizing her hand he tried to hasten her steps homeward, a strange look of perplexity still puckering his baby brows. Suddenly a light broke over his face, and darting to a flower-bed, he gathered the bright blossoms ruthlessly with both hands at a time, stems and blooms and delicate trailing roots in his vigorous grasp, and eagerly running back, with a face all sunshine, he showered them over his mother's feet, calling to her triumphantly in her own sweet language, which they always spoke together, "*Madonna mia !*"

It had been very quiet at the château during those days of the early childhood of little
Felix, for the count and his young wife
belonged to the *haute noblesse*, which in those
days, so closely following upon the Revolution, scarcely deserved the usual English inter-
pretation of privileged class. Their circle had
been painfully decimated by death and cramped
by confiscation; and although now, since the
soldier-ruler of the land was beginning to
dream of a court more magnificent than that
of his Bourbon predecessors, he was slowly
restoring the lands and revenues to those
nobles whose favor he desired to win, this
circle was still widely pervaded by sadness
and restraint, and the Count and Countess de
Montal could have been but heavy-hearted in
the gayety of the growing court of the First
Consul and his gracious Josephine, had there
been no deeper sorrow of their own to live
above.

Thus it was not strange that the beautiful
Hôtel Montal, in the Faubourg St. Germain,
stood closed and desolate ; for the Consul, in

his eagerness to attach to himself and his growing fortunes all who might by their distinction of birth, of manner, and of education supply the elements which he knew he could not create, was imperative in his orders that those he designated should constantly attend him. And Monsieur de Rémusat, who was at this time prefect of the palace, a wise and unfailing guide in all matters of etiquette and of court-ceremonial, and to whom, in these early days of his grandeur, Napoleon always deferred, had signified that Monsieur and Madame de Montal were not only to be sought, but also to be conciliated; and the countess, to whom the *gaucheries* of the parvenu court were distasteful, had found that she might not absent herself with impunity when Madame Bonaparte received. So the mere suggestion, rumor-wise, that Madame de Montal, the wife of the senator, was to be named lady-in-waiting to Josephine, hastened her decision to withdraw from Paris to their country-seat of Val-Maria, and make of it their permanent home.

Josephine, with her infinite tact and delicate appreciation of the sympathies of her high-born friend, shrank from urging her attendance at the Tuileries, and manœuvred to avert the storm which threatened to break upon the head of the fair young countess, who, though much younger, had been inti-mate with Josephine as Madame de Beau-harnais, and had, during the Directory, been an *habitué* of the charming salon of Madame Bonaparte in the Rue Chantereine while the general of the Army of Italy was winning his brilliant victories at Dego, Mondovi, and Milan. The influence of Josephine with her imperious husband was then at its height; thus, when Madame de Rémusat saw fit to urge upon the Consul to remember how useful it might be to him to number among his friends in the Sen-ate one of such distinguished position, ability, and influence, with such gifts of manner and of oratory as the Count de Montal possessed, he controlled his impatience under the thwart-ing, and suffered himself to be conciliated. The countess was not named lady-in-waiting, but received in lieu of the appointment a gracious note from Josephine, regretting her withdrawal from Paris, with a charming reminder that the private salon of her old friend was always open to her in the Tuileries, as it had been in the hôtel of the Rue de Chantereine.

Affairs of this kind did not invariably terminate so happily in the days of the Consulate and Empire, for the man who became accustomed to bend kingdoms to his sway found an extraordinary leisure for the smallest details of his court, and would not tolerate the least resistance to his tyrannical will.

As for Monsieur de Montal, aristocrat though he was by birth and endowment, his education and the strong Christian bent of his character had made of him, at heart, a lover of men : whether as patriot for his country or, in a larger sense, for his race, he scarcely knew in the early days of his career, when life lay open to him, beckoning him to choose his field of influence. His extraordinary powers of eloquence, even then, gave

c

him promise of mastery over men, and his
devotion to his church, and his intimate
friendship with some of the finer minds
among the priests, with whom he often dis-
cussed the deeper problems of life and man's
relation to them and to the Infinite, led him
to ask himself seriously, in a period of youthful religious enthusiasm, if he should not become a priest and put himself in the way of
suffering for his faith. "But no," he con-
cluded, with a characteristic confession of self-
study and self-knowledge, not ignoring those
propensities of his nature which to him, in
that visionary age, seemed decidedly human
rather than intrinsically noble, and thus the
decision cost him the more, for it was a confession that he found the world with its rapid
movement of life full of attraction. And for
a time he waited the issue, stirring up public
sentiment in the direction of his chivalrous
impulses by his pen, or by vehement orations
which early won for him a name. With his
intense love of liberty, his scorn of oppression,
his sympathy with the needs of the poor, his

absolute graciousness to those beneath him in
rank and fortune, among whom he had many
loyal and beloved friends whom he received
with the greatest tenderness and courtesy,
it was nevertheless true that he had all his
life a horror of the sway of democracy ; that
he believed in an aristocratic government, and
that he never ceased to retain his visionary
admiration for his own class, judging it for
practical purposes, too much as a woman or
a poet judges, from self-consciousness; and
out of his own lofty estimate of the duties
and responsibilities of that class, repeating
often to himself the motto carved over the
quaint fireplace of the hall of Val-Maria *" Noblesse oblige."* It seemed to him no hardship
that the people should be ruled by such a
body of men as he told himself the nobles
ought to be.

While yet a very young man, and while the
memory of the Reign of Terror was still vivid,
he had caused his friends great anxiety by the
publication in one of the provincial papers of
an intolerant article called out by the rumor

that a certain general, stationed in Paris, had refused to admit to his regiment the sons of noble families who had proffered him their services. He asks, "why the new government had divided sympathies, proclaiming itself the enemy of half the nation?" "And what has made us your enemies?" he asks, angrily. "Is it because we write a *de* before our names, or because we make the sign of a cross when we enter a church? Then your liberty is nothing but a lying and cruel oppression!"

But, fortunately, this was in the early days of the Directory, when a brighter atmosphere was beginning to dawn over France; there was not always time to punish the utterances of discontent, for the government was beginning to occupy itself with reconstruction rather than in seeking out offences. In fact, one of the five in whom the supreme power was vested thus outlined to a colleague the new pacific policy: "We must let them talk about politics as they please; we ought to be more liberal than the Convention; they undertook to coerce the thoughts of men, but it is the duty of the Directory to give the mind free scope. It is, perhaps, the surest means of ascertaining public opinion, and of remedying those evils into which an abuse of power may betray us."

The knowledge of this greater freedom of speech and more catholic spirit in the heads of the government tempted Monsieur de Montal to emerge from his provincial seclusion and return to Paris for a while, merely as an onlooker, taking up his abode in the Hôtel Montal, in the Faubourg St. Germain, which had been vacant since the death of his father, many years before, and which therefore required much expenditure of time and thought in its re-establishment, before it should be fit for the reception of the young wife who had remained with their infant child in their country home.

Meanwhile, it was an absorbing fascination to one of his statesman-like and philanthropic proclivities to watch the intricacies of this great drama of government which was being performed, without previous rehearsal, on a stage subject to upheavals, with new actors ever taking up the important *rôles*, before a people of whose applause there could be no certainty.

There was something in the acquaintance of both Carnot and Barras, the more important members of the Directory, to attract the young Count de Montal, who accepted with pleasure the unusual advances made to him by Monsieur Carnot, whose quiet home-circle and philosophic talk offered a strange and welcome contrast to the excitement and splendor of Paris, where this austere student seemed almost an anomaly. That so staunch a republican should be quite indifferent to the dignity of his "directorial purple" was easy to comprehend; but that one who had turned his profound studies to such advantage that his advice on all matters within the province of the Directory was confessed to be ever the wisest, could satisfy his conscience by giving his signature, as a mere matter of form, to decrees of which he knew nothing, as often happened, was more difficult to account for.

Sometimes, in the quiet of his study, when the philosopher had forgotten himself and the presence of his guest, to wax eloquent over some absorbing theme, the young aristocrat, listening in delight, would suddenly remember with a thrill of horror, "This man sat in judgment over Louis XVI. !" And then he would ask himself, " How can he ever again yield himself calmly to these intellectual abstractions? Does such impassivity belong to age, or only to this strange period?" And it would seem to him, as he sat restlessly waiting for a pause in which he might escape and be alone with himself, that the eloquent words were no longer more than the dust and ashes of a decoying and deceiving fire. He could find no beauty in them, no hope ; they became terrible to him, with his burning love of truth and beauty, because they bore the semblance of a noble reality ; and this condemnation of the unhappy king was a crime he was not yet old enough, nor dispassionate enough, to forgive Carnot.

At such moments his fierce young nature

rose up in rebellion, and Paris, the brilliant city, seemed to him a hell, a capital without religion, a people truly divided against itself, —the upper half, the wealthy class, living in reckless gayety; the other, the people over whom his generous soul yearned, besieging the bakers' shops with long hours of patient waiting, for a few ounces of miserable, dark bread, weighed off with discreet economy, so much for each mouth of the household, to the cry of " Your certificates, messieurs!"

Your certificates! your sworn statement of numbers, lest we sell you too much—for words are but base coin in times like these! It made him ill at heart; but how was it all to end? From whence should help come?

Sometimes he wrote himself calm, in passionate protestations, in midnight vigils in his solitary hôtel in the Faubourg St. Germain, publishing his unsigned articles in some provincial paper, for at least he was beginning to learn discretion in Paris, not from fear, but from the assured conviction that God had given him his talents to use in His service, and he must be wise in this his strange generation—the Reign of Terror was not so long past!

Yet sometimes he grew desperate with the wish to scatter something from his superfluity among the underfed masses; he dared not do it rashly, and fearing that his youthful impetuosity needed some restraint, he broached his project of concerted help by the aristocracy in one of the long-closed salons, whose gracious mistress, dignified, silver-haired, and saddened by the events of the past years, was beginning once more to gather friends about her.

She shook her head imperatively; but she gave him her tapering white hand with a warm grasp of admiration. "A modest largesse, with a quiet, unknown hand," she said; "in these times we cannot do more, we few who have not been despoiled. We must wait! And, meanwhile, it is better than the Convention."

"It is much better," declared a young officer, who stood by. "One can live on little, if the heart is gay ! And they have still the strength—these people for whom you weep—to visit the theatres and applaud to the skies ' The Abolition of Royalty' or the ' Apotheosis of Marat.' Life goes not so badly for them."

With Barras, Louis de Montal felt that he had more in common ; for this director was known to favor the return of the Bourbons, and to pretend that the Directory was to prepare the way for this event. He found the audiences of this ruler intensely interesting, as his salons were not only the centre of the political movement of the time, but were frequently rendered pathetic by the appeals of disinterested friends for the recall of some noble family from banishment, or for the restoration of lands and revenues to others who had been despoiled. More than once he had seen a petition presented by the gracious and systematic Madame de Beauharnais, who came more often than others on these kindly missions, and whose heart in these days, as in later ones, was with the Royalists and with .

those to whom she felt that power belonged
by divine right.

If at times Barras appeared too much the
friend of all parties to direct his power by any
fixed principle, he was still an enigma, and a
most interesting one, and in his salon the hope
of France—its fate at least—seemed to centre.
Here Louis de Montal first met the man upon
whom all eyes were turning, the young Cor-
sican general, Napoleon Bonaparte, of whom
Barras thought most highly, though the other
directors disliked him and spoke contemptu-
ously of "the little leather breeches."

Perhaps this very contempt first occasioned
the knightly Montal, with his scorn of injustice,
to turn his attention to the study of this new
and unique figure, for whose oddity, brusque-
ness, and ignorance of all polite forms some
allowance was necessary.   But it was not long
before the general, as chief of the Army of
Italy, had signally distinguished himself, and
Montal, watching with keen interest, not only
realized how varied were the gifts and grasp of
the victorious soldier, but gave him credit for

an absorbed and disinterested love for France, which finally overcame his reluctance to take part in the great political struggle of his time ; and scarcely confessing to himself that he was already counting upon Bonaparte as the saviour of his country, he accepted the appointment of senator, which came to him later, throwing himself enthusiastically into every real question that came up for debate.

And this man, with the mighty intellect and magnificent projects centred upon the prosperity of France, was he to be their leader?

CHAPTER FOURTH.

THERE was indeed much time for this ideal culture of the boy to which the countess devoted herself, for since the days of the old *régime* life had been very quiet at the Château of Val-Maria. "Too quiet!" grumbled the villagers, as the distant echo of the fêtes of the gay capital reached their ears; for they too liked the occasional chance of grumbling at overwork instead of stagnation, and the excitement of holding an indignation meeting, as they were doing just now in the little square, to relate to each other how Monsieur Charles, the grand *chef-de-cuisine* at the château, had not been satisfied with

45

the best fruit of their gardens, "because he
was in a humor *impossible* to please!" And
how he had sent word to Jacques, who had
been growing *choux-fleurs* all his life, that they
should be "white" the next time he brought
them to serve to such guests, as if one could
find much whiter than the *choux-fleurs* of
Jacques! It was quite possible that German
Karl, the vegetable cook, might have his head
turned too by such grand company, coming
from such a barbarous Protestant country, and
not being used to the *grands seigneurs*, and
forget to put milk in the pot, all to bring dis-
grace on Jacques!

"And then there had been pâtés from
Paris, with ornaments to make you afraid!"
interposed Henri, the vender of sabots.

But Pierre, who could be magnanimous,
feeling himself the great man of the village—
Pierre confessed that these pâtés were "truly
divine." There had been no occasion, in his
day, for such pâtés in Val-Maria, or he could
show them! But he had studied them, these
pâtés, he had studied them well, when he had

helped Monsieur Charles to unpack them ; and
to-morrow he would show them a wonder—
a pâté—but such a one as they had never
tasted ! And this they should all eat in the
square, with some good *vin-du-pays*, for
Madame la Comtesse made announcement by
him that to-morrow, at four o'clock, there
should be a supper for the villagers, with
"friandises" from the château, and he, Pierre,
would furnish the pâté ! "Come then, my
malcontents !"

Thus it was always Pierre who made himself of consequence ; he had much time for
talking and he was not lazy with his tongue ;
and he went often to the château to arrange
affairs with Monsieur Charles. For Monsieur
Charles had quite particular ideas about the
shapes of the little cakes for the table of Madame
la Comtesse, thinking each day that, if they
were different, madame might give them more
attention, for, as it was now, it was scarcely
worth while to serve them at all ! And truly,
he, Pierre, led the life of a dog to suit the
whims of Monsieur Charles ; verily he thought

sometimes he would enlist and finish all this tumult about little cakes!

" Wait, then, till we have well eaten our pâté, we others!" shouted a chorus of jubilant voices, for fêtes had been rare, of late, in Val-Maria.

"Or, well, for the conscription, my son," recommended old Jean, placidly, with the air of one who seldom spoke, but who knew his subject well, having much time for listening and thinking, as he sat in the door-way of his shop, day after day, patching the working blouses of the men, or now and then making a new one, "The conscription comes also to Val-Maria, and that is soon enough for thee!"

So it was one day grumbling because it was too quiet; and another, grumbling because their old-fashioned ways did not suit the grand staff of servants at the château, when the village-help was required; and the next day, maybe, placid to stagnation, not even an apple falling from a tree, and everything going on peacefully, and the Madonna keeping everything

in order, that was what you might expect in
Val-Maria! And then the discontent would
begin again, just for a change, or there would
come news, and everybody wanted something
to happen, and nobody knew what it should
be, except Pierre, who would have it one thing
on Thursday and another on Friday; and it
was confusing, indeed, to keep one's head
in such times! It had always been that way
in Val-Maria since the days of the Bourbons.

Monsieur le Curé was growing silver-haired
and infirm; he had learned his politics in the
days of the old *régime*, and he could not rouse
himself to a comprehension of this state of
things. He was glad to leave the harangues
to Monsieur l'Abbé, who was a learned gentle-
man, quite capable of comprehending these
strange new times. The politics of the father
of Monsieur le Comte sufficed for a quiet old
curé, who had no part in the affairs of the great
world, and there was no time to change them
now. "To love one's neighbor, and to do
one's work, like children of the good God,"

that was his creed, under one *régime* or another, it mattered not!

So he did not often linger under the willows when Pierre unfolded his news—it was a distraction from better things—for his time was not very long, and there were the children to teach, and many sweet old legends and histories of the Saints to be conned, for sometimes, now, he feared his memory was growing vague. So he more often shook his head in mild deprecation, when there was much talk in the square, and turned aside for a stroll down the river bank, meditating upon some holy theme which seemed to come to him the better for the mere touch of the quaint old volume he carried with him, rarely opened, for he had eyesight for but little reading now. His tall figure was slightly bowed over the cane he was beginning to depend upon to stay his slackening footsteps; his long, thin silver locks flowed back from his benevolent bronzed face, under the black three-cornered hat; only his dark, kind eyes looked out from the features— once rough, but now changed, sharpened by age and spiritualized by his holy life—with the glow and charm of youth; for, as years passed, the creed of the good curé had grown more simple and loving, and the beauty of his heart was in his eyes.

Some of the older peasants could have told you his name, but if you had asked the children for Monsieur Simon, even on Sunday, they would have smiled up at you with blank, rosy faces, answering "savons-pas," we do not know, though Monsieur le Curé had but just left his touch of benediction on their sunburnt locks.

Sometimes, when Pierre had talked more than was good for his peace, Monsieur l'Abbé would come over the bridge from the château and make it all quite plain to them that everything was going well; that France was prosperous beyond all past times; that they should all thank heaven that so great a man as the First Consul was their chief ruler. Had he not opened the churches for the people? Had he not constantly shown the highest consideration for the clergy, reinstating them in their dignities? Might they not read in the *Moniteur* of yesterday, that now, in his journey through Belgium, the one who accompanied him to do him highest honor—considered and attended like the prince he was—was none other than his Highness, the Cardinal Caprara? "And is it not the first time since the Revolution that we can say our religion is re-established? Come, then, my children, forget not to give thanks, and to pray for our victorious Consul."

And then Monsieur Felix, who was often with his tutor when he made his speeches to the admiring crowd—little Felix, now a beautiful boy of six, who had been listening eagerly with glowing cheeks and sparkling eyes to the harangue—would burst out impetuously like an inspired orator, "My friends, we must *love* Napoleon. He is very great, and brave, and noble, and he loves France!"

And once when Monsieur l'Abbé paused for breath, the little fellow bounded upon the old stone bench under the willows, his bright hair blowing about his spirited

face as he tossed off his plumed cap, shouting with an enthusiasm that carried his
audience by storm, "I love him! He is my
hero!"

It was quite true; for now it was more
than two years since the beautiful Parian bust
of this wonderful leader of men had held a
place of honor in the apartment of the boy,
on a pedestal draped with rich crimson velvet
by the countess's own hands; and lately a
little curtain had been placed behind it, against
which the noble outlines showed in clearer
relief, for beyond all his treasures Felix prized
this beautiful head.

It had first taken possession of the little
artist's soul by its beauty; but his heart was
so tender, his childish imagination so vivid,
and his temperament so strangely poetic—his
unusual training, withal, leading him always
to associate the higher inward beauty with
every outward manifestation—that gradually
this bust became to him like a living friend,
passionately adored for every noble quality the
perfect lineaments seemed to indicate; and

later, as years passed, endowed, in his generous and undiscriminating belief, with whatever attributes of loftiness the world's truest
heroes had possessed.

He talked to it as if it could answer him
back; his lessons with his tutor, his daily experiences and fanciful visions of greatness;
above all, his growing acquaintance with the
characters of the great men of the past—an
acquaintance which opened very early for the
child, because of his father's unusual fund of
historic knowledge and the use he made of
it in training his son—all these came to be
shared with the unresponsive marble friend
around whom the boy's growing, enriching
life had so strangely centred.

Yet, in a certain sense, this friend was not
unresponsive. It was he who enforced every
lesson; he who fostered the child's memory;
above all, he who, growing day by day in the
boy's noble soul-growth, held constantly before him the lofty ideal of a manhood regal
with every virtue his youthful imagination
could conceive, and crowned with every gift

of intellect of which so boyish a worshipper might dream.

And for the face—was it not very beautiful, as the face of one so great and good should be? How could one see it and not love?

CHAPTER FIFTH.

HE count, who was obliged to be much in Paris during the session of the Senate, found his wife growing paler each time that he returned from the capital; or it might be—for love admits slight pretexts—it might be only that the singular spirituality of her face struck him more vividly after these short absences; it could not be that a few days had changed her, for he never left her for any length of time.

"I will give up the Senate, my wife," he said with infinite tenderness. "It will be better for you, and we will go away for a long time; perhaps to Florence."

56

"Oh, Louis, no! We cannot leave Val-Maria; it is best for Felix; he is so happy here! And you would feel laid aside without your life at the Senate; you would be unhappy. And you are needed there."

He shook his head in deprecation which might not have been playful. He was beginning to question the value of individuals in that august body of France which he had entered, two years before, with such exalted hopes and aims, as he had already doubted his own fitness for the position; for with sympathies warm for the needs of his nation, and a conscience that was semi-English, he felt that all countries which aspired to freedom or sought for its equivalent in a government based upon the welfare of its people, should encourage the bold pleading of all great causes before its public tribunals. But sometimes he fancied he detected a strange paralysis of will in the words and actions of men who had hitherto seemed to him great; it was as if some mastering force swayed them in a direction uncomprehended by themselves, and his whole soul rebelled, for to one of his mind great results could not be compassed with closed eyes.

"There shall be no changes that do not please you," he said, "yet I should like a little change at Val-Maria. You are over-strained with incessant dwelling upon this one brooding thought; this tension must be broken by duties not so dear. We must see friends occasionally; it is growing dull for you."

"Not with you and Felix," she pleaded. "You know I want nothing more."

"But if it is not wise? sweet mother of our child."

The pet name, added after a moment's pause, said so much to her it could not be resisted; naming her objection and refuting it at once.

"It will be best for Felix, too," he said when she had acquiesced and they had talked together of those whom the count should bring with him on his return from Paris. "His mind is so awake, and his love is so keen, that I have seen him watch your dear face furtively and almost with a look of pain. He will be so proud of his mother among her guests !

" And afterwards we will have much time to ourselves," he continued, wishing to re-assure her with what she liked best, for his heart was heavier about her than over Felix. "Our Consul goes for a tour of conquest through Belgium in a few days, with Joseph-ine, duly attended—a cardinal in his suite. After that there will be nothing for the Senate to do until we are called together by the President to prepare a triumphant address of welcome."

She was surprised at his tone and looked up anxiously. "What is it, Louis? You have changed."

" Oh, no, I have not changed," he answered, lightly. "If anything has changed it is not I ! Sometimes I think I am too stable, too posi-tive, for these times of change. I am not sure that I like the thought of Cardinal Caprara attending on the movements of General Bonaparte, nor to see his wife at the Tuileries in a state so much greater than my own would keep."

"Dear Louis, you are not jealous! We do not care for state."

"No, my beloved one; we do not indeed. If it ended with the pleasure to them, it would not matter. But it has its meaning. Sometimes I wonder if it is all wise, if the people trust too much!"

Thus it chanced that the château, which had so long seemed almost to sleep amid its stately gardens and groves, put on a brighter air of welcome to receive the group of guests who came with the count from Paris, the day of the meeting in the little square of Val-Maria. The banqueting-hall, long disused, was re-opened; and here, amid its too florid decorations of scroll-work and gilding, and roses and loves, untouched since the early time of the Renaissance, the gracious countess seemed a fairer thing than ever, with her lovely face and her unworldly ways.

A Florentine sculptor of great reputation,

who had been invited by the Consul to visit
Paris, was among this group of friends. He
was intimate with the family of the countess
in Florence, and was looking forward with
pleasure to the meeting promised him by the
count, not only because he had known her in
her girlhood, but because he had heard of her
beauty, and the count was eager to have a
marble bust of his wife when Signore Alfonte
should sufficiently have studied her face to
undertake the work.

In the moment of greeting there had been a
flush on her pale face which slightly modified
its habitual sadness, and of her beauty there
could be no question. But as the unusual
glow of animation wore away, the artist was
disappointed, and indignant with himself that
he could think of nothing but a *mater dolo-
rosa*, as he furtively watched the exquisite
face of his unconscious hostess. The pale-
rose satin court-dress, with its jewelled bands
of ruby and pearl, was not inappropriate to the
count's young wife; but the pure sanctity of
the brow and eyes, which seemed to tell of a

6

great pain, borne through a greater love, would have seemed nearer to his ideal had she appeared more fittingly clothed in simple garments without form or fashion, flowing into lines of grace with her queenly motions, and whiter than her pale face when the flush had passed.

His artist soul had seized the presence of a mystery which he felt it impossible to fathom, as he watched the mistress of this beautiful home, and recalled the tones of profound tenderness in which the count had spoken of his wife: to him, with his history of utter desolation, this home-life seemed to offer such incalculable riches!

At dinner the talk was brilliant, and it was impossible to permit himself to be absorbed by this single thought; but when they passed into the drawing-room, and the countess moved about among her guests, the fascination became irresistible, and he forgot his interest in the topic he had himself broached—of the state of art in France—for he noticed that she was growing restless and distrait, turning her eyes frequently towards the long windows that opened on the terrace, with an air of expectancy that was almost painful. The banquet had been interminable to her; she was unaccustomed of late to these long society hours, and it seemed to her that she could not wait for Felix, who was to come to them in the drawing-room when dinner was over; to her morbid fancy this first break in the quiet of their idyllic life was almost like an infidelity to Felix, who had always been with them at this hour, and now she was waiting breathlessly for him to come.

Her husband stepped quickly to her side with a whispered word of reassurance, for he, too, found the waiting long, and as she turned more calmly, quieted by his tender comprehension, her whole face became suddenly transfused with a passionate love-light and content, as Felix came bounding towards her and was clasped for an instant in her longing arms.

But in that moment the artist had fathomed his mystery. This radiant child was the source

of her anguish and its cure ; her whole being
was wrapped in his. He never forgot that
beautiful group of mother and child, as he first
saw it through a mist that seemed to swim
before his eyes and dim the rich coloring and
the perfect outlines to the vagueness and ideality of a dream. The faces and the attitudes
were perfect models for the group he dreamed
of leaving to the world as his great work, his
group of *Mother-Love,* which had. dwelt in his
heart ceaselessly as the divine passion, ever
since he had roused himself to interest in his
art, after those dark days which brought him
his desolation—the loss of his wife and their
infant child.

The count had been eagerly watching for
the impression his wife should produce upon
his friend, who had given him no promise in
regard to the bust which he so eagerly desired.
To his continued insistence but one answer had
been returned : " My friend, my time is not
my own; it belongs to my art; and I am
studying still—though I am no longer young—
for the great work of my life. I shall take

no more portraits unless the face moves me in the direction of my ideal. Beyond my art, life holds nothing for me."

" Madonna. mia! you are so beautiful to-night!" the eager words in a caressing, childish voice broke in upon his revery, as the countess came towards him leading little Felix by the hand; and with a mighty effort he brought himself back to the claims of the moment, as he tried to ingratiate himself with the beautiful child, who was truly a delight for the eyes of an artist, in his gala suit of crimson velvet and rare old lace.

The count had observed his absorption with satisfaction. " That is how they spoil each other!" he said, lightly, to his friend, as his wife's attention was claimed by another group. "But you look as if you had already chosen your pose."

" Ah, yes; there is but one possible for her. We must have them both: without the boy she is not herself. It shall be a great work! We must have the figure, too, for there is meaning in her motion as in her face; the impression is not complete unless her movement is suggested, and the boy shall be always with her when I work. It shall be just as I have seen it, only the draperies more noble, and lilies instead of jewels. But later we will talk of it—not here."

" You recall me to my duty as host," Montal said, turning with him in the direction of the terrace.

" No, no; it is not that we may not talk; you do not understand me—and what can be more beautiful than art? It is only that I cannot! For me it means too much, and we must be alone. My friend, you are blessed indeed. I have my art, but I have nothing else; and to-night it comes over me like a passion !"

The three were alone in the middle of the great drawing-room, and the words seemed to have been wrung from him in a moment of uncontrollable emotion. No answer was possible. As one who knows that life brings moments that must be borne alone, his friend wrung his hand with a convulsive pressure, and without a look or a word, hastened for-

ward to join the others on the terrace, leaving
his boy beside him.

The sensitive child, with all his holier instincts prematurely quickened by his unusual
training, knew that some great pain must be
hidden in the words he had overheard without
fully understanding; he hesitated only for a
moment, and then pressing closer, with quick,
caressing movements of his childish fingers on
the hand that had been dropped just within
his reach, he looked up into the artist's face
with the whole wealth of his soul shining in
his glorious spirit-eyes.

"Mon ami—mon *cher* ami!" he cried, "I
love you!"

CHAPTER SIXTH.

ITTLE Felix flitted about on the moon-
lit terrace, coming and going from
group to group, now and then pausing to listen with delight as he caught the
name of his hero; if seldom seizing the full
intent of the speaker, yet retaining a vivid
impression that he had become a sort of demi-
god upon whom the fortunes of France depended.

Meanwhile the conversation was animated,
as the shades of opinion were sufficiently
diverse to give it sparkle. Several of Montal's
colleagues in the Senate had returned with
him, and one of them was giving an enthu-

siastic account of the "Résumé of the condition of the Republic," recently laid before the
Corps Législatif.

"To name only a few of the points," he
said, rising impetuously, and almost forgetting,
in his excitement, that he was not addressing
"the House." "First, there was peace with
foreign powers ; a partition of Germany recognized by all the sovereigns! The Swiss
Constitution ; the Concordat! Regulation of
public education ; the Institute of France ;
improved administration of justice; improved
condition of finances; the civil code. Monsieur André, you helped to pass upon some
of its provisions when it came before the
Assembly ; you know how the prodigious intellectual grasp of the man came out! Then
we have public works in France and on the
frontiers : plans for Mont Cenis and the banks
of the Rhine; the Canal d'Oureq; Elba; St. Do-
mingo ; proposals of laws to cover every interest
in the Republic, without limit! Indirect taxa-
tion ; chambers of commerce ; manufactures ;
laws for the exercise of the medical profession ;

and so on. It is gigantic. And as to the enthusiasm !———"

" What should one expect but enthusiasm, when it is all true? Not written on paper, but in responsive France. The people are not ingrates !"

" You are right, my friend," said Monsieur André, warmly. " If there have been grumblers because we have a soldier at the head of a royal nation, it is because the day of fools is not past ; but they have learned, at least, that discipline at the top means discipline in rank and file, right down through the core of the nation!

" Another *on-dit:* the army grumbles now and then because they have not all the honors ; but what difference does that make to us? This is what the men who *know* say of our Soldier-Consul (Monsieur de Vaublanc, in the Corps Législatif, word for word ; I was there and heard him speak) : ' What chief of a nation has ever shown a greater love of peace?' Furor impossible to describe !"

" Deputations to Saint-Cloud of devotion

and congratulation from our body," said another senator; "a day of prosperity for France!"

"And of glory for the man who *makes* France," said another voice, rounding the sentence which had been simply finished with a point of profound admiration. "Montal, your eloquence is in repose to-night."

"To leave a place courteous for that of my guests," responded Montal, with an attempt to rouse himself more completely from the meditative mood in which his talk with Alfonte had plunged him. "Monsieur André, you spoke of the 'soldier at the head of a royal nation.' Was it a word of chance or an enigma?"

"As you please, and for you to explain; at one time you saw much of General Bonaparte. We are all friends, and the subject is large and interesting."

"I know nothing, absolutely nothing," the count declared with emphasis.

"Precisely; in the Senate, of course, one knows whatever may be convenient, or what-

ever may have been declared," said an old
nobleman who had been listening in silence;
"but otherwheres one has opinions. There
was a rumor in Paris, in the Faubourg, not
so long since, of a promise from General
Bonaparte to Barras, as to the final recall of
the old dynasty when the way should be
prepared. And Madame Bonaparte espouses
that cause openly."

"Barras has confessed as much to me,"
Montal acknowledged. "But even yesterday
is 'long since' in our times, and from the
Directory to the Consulate is longer still,
though it took but an hour to make the
transit."

"But Madame Bonaparte is always charming, always 'sympathique;' she pleads for
all in distress," said a white-haired dowager
who knew both the court and the Faubourg.
"And if there are too many deprivations for
the share of the Royalists, it is a strength the
more for our party; so the Consul knows
how to listen ! It was the Little General who
pleaded in the days of the Directory, and

Madame de Beauharnais who coquetted. She is our hope."

"Excuse me, my dear, if I am not so sanguine," said the old marquis; "but a word which the Consul has recently dropped has come to me quite faithfully: '*I am the man of the State; I am the French Revolution.*'"

"Through Madame de Rémusat?" queried one of the group, after an instant's pause of consternation. "For at the Tuileries there are not too many epigrams. The talk is like ice, with a snow of reserve to hide the glitter! One is taught what one may speak, and it is easier for those who have thoughts to keep silence. It is always Madame de Rémusat who makes the Consul talk more freely; she is so young, so witty, so simple, so wise, so discreet, and so entirely *aristocrate!* It was almost a *coup d'état* to secure Monsieur and Madame de Rémusat for the new court at the Tuileries, and the Consul is proud of it yet. Sometimes he actually converses with the first lady-in-waiting."

"But in the next room one hears nothing,"

D 7

said the old marquis. "If such a word has wings, it was spoken to be heard."

"It is charged, you think, with a mission for La Vendée?" his wife suggested.

"I can give you a better one," interposed Montal, who was growing uneasy at the tone of the conversation. "And for my authority, —I had it from Monsieur de Talleyrand.— Felix, come here; listen to a word you may learn by heart, for it was spoken by your hero. 'The man who has courage, the man who serves his country, the man who illustrates his character by great deeds, has no need of ancestors; he is of himself everything.' Now go, my boy, to Signore Alfonte, who is beckoning to you. How say you, Monsieur le Marquis? If a new aristocracy is to be created from the people, it is at least a noble thought to base it on such a foundation."

"Your word does more honor to the Consul than mine," the marquis returned, courteously; "but I leave it to madame to judge whether it requires greater gifts to make it conform to the conduct of the extraordinary man who first uttered them."

"I have been too little at court to have opinions," the countess answered, with a smile.

"Pardon, *ma chère;* we were saying before you joined us," explained the marquis, turning towards Madame de Montal, "that only those who are not at court can afford the luxury of opinions at all. There was an effort to push opinions—innocent ones, on literary matters—two or three weeks ago at the Tuileries. General Bonaparte had decided that it was time to begin to gather men of letters at the reunions of Madame Bonaparte; for no one can deny that he has a most marvellously comprehensive brain—our Consul; nothing is forgotten; and a vigilance upon all this machinery he sets in motion—a vigilance which is scarcely human! No one thinks for himself, but every one does *his* bidding, and in the end it is as well to let one's brain rest, for the Consul has enough for all, and keeps it always going."

"But about these literary receptions?"

"Well, the first one goes off charmingly. Monsieur de Rémusat sends the invitations; there were the new Lyceums to talk of; the collection of French paintings just placed at the Musée; above all, the pensions and rewards just decreed to men of letters; with a fair sprinkling of academicians and savants—it was an inspiring change for some of us weary ones; and to crown all, Bonaparte himself, in a good humor and really brilliant."

"I am so glad for Josephine's sake!" the countess exclaimed, with keen interest. "You know her salon in the Rue Chantereine was charming, but at the Tuileries it has always seemed different."

"A difference with a reason, my dear! Of course we come a second time a little freer of movement, like birds who have tried our wings. We talk among ourselves with more *élan.* The Consul is late. We are in the second salon, where Madame Bonaparte cannot hear: some one remembers Monsieur de Lille, and the question goes, if it would not be a little triumph to charm him back to the court from his quiet rooms across the Seine, and whether he could be made to accept the honors he has declined, since our literary evenings may make us worthier of his society. Suddenly the Consul appears. Something has vexed him, or he is seriously arranging some weighty matter of state; but he looks at us under his eyebrows quite silently, and the whole atmosphere changes. The Abbé Morellet perceives nothing, and has the misfortune to wax eloquent on your theme, Monsieur de Montal—liberty of thought and speech, and the advantages it secures for nations! It is a pretty theme when its surroundings are made for it like a frame; but at last Monsieur l'Abbé discovers that he has talked for an interminable time, and no one has answered anything but a few little, freezing words."

" But surely Madame Bonaparte was there; and you, who can always talk, my dear marquise, why did you not say something for the honor of the court? The Consul cannot

always be free for the thoughts of the moment ; it is inconceivable !"

" My dear, we were all of us there, and we
could none of us talk. I give you my word !
In the Faubourg we are quite capable of
whatever you please : that is the extraordinary
influence of the man ! Whatever he will not
do, we may not do. If he is absorbed, we
may not shine. But pardon me if I fatigue
you : I am giving you the history of a ' movement,' for it positively has that importance.

" Third evening : everybody thinks of the
Abbé de Lille and the Abbé Morellet ; and
nobody makes mistakes, because nobody talks;
and every one tries to smile, enough to hide
the mortal fatigue, and not enough to look as
if we were thinking about anything in particular ; for opinions were not *en règle* for this
famous evening ; and the savants are out of
place ; and we are out of place ; and the Consul is preoccupied and appears to notice nothing.   And this is the glorious finale of our
' soirées littéraires.'   For of course there
went forth a decree to Monsieur de Rémusat."

" I do not understand it at all," the countess exclaimed. "One must have moments of absorption, and for one at the head of a government!—The wonder is that he can give any attention to these details."

" My dear, you are very young, as Monsieur de Talleyrand remarks to Madame de Rémusat, who still permits herself emotions. But that is the man! Everybody else may have moments of absorption without results. We women of the Court of France might be capable of directing a salon, if it were not decreed that we should not. The whole thing explains itself by the Consul's objection to Madame de Staël: 'This woman teaches people to think who never thought before.' And now, when Louis Bonaparte will not keep away from her salons, although the Consul has forbidden his attendance—for the discussion is free upon all political subjects—our Monsieur Louis Bonaparte is watched, by order of the Consul!"

"Rumor is not always candid—not always exact," the countess said, with a feeling of depression, "and I think you are very hard upon the Consul. Every one acknowledges his magnetism."

"I grant you his magnetism, my dear countess; he is as magnetic as an infernal machine! As for me, I do not like this modern kind of sorcery. It reminds me of this curious invention our academicians were raving over not long ago—'electricity,' I believe they call it. My own son was one of them, as crazy as the rest, and they were all in my salon discussing their scheme for carrying the new power—no one knows how far—through a tube under one of the basins of the Tuileries. They had a queer-looking little machine of glass, and wire coils, and Victor was charmingly polite. 'It shall be madame my mother who touches it the first,' he said, bringing me a little handle at the end of a cord. I give you my word, I was at the other end of the room from his innocent-looking box, but I never felt such a thrill! Pouf! and after that I was numb! 'It's the kind of work the Little Corporal likes, and no good will come of introducing it,' I told Victor. But it seems the savants have known about it for a long time, and the English are more learned than we in this kind of foolishness. I confess I owe them no grudge for it; and all the more because it makes the little man at our end gnash his teeth."

"My dear marquise," the young countess pleaded.

"My dear countess, would it be *drôle*, do you think, if the Little Corporal got hold of the end that pricks? and—*allons*, we are all of us discreet, and I really must tell you my discovery. You see the Consul thinks himself superior to everybody else, but he is always afraid of superiority in others! It is so simple that it is almost naïve; but I like the Consul better for it: it makes him more human."

"Signore Alfonte must tell us what he thinks of this beginning of art-culture in France, of which Monsieur de Montal has seen something since I have left Paris," the countess suggested, eagerly seizing the oppor-

f

tunity of introducing a new subject, as the artist came up the steps of the terrace refreshed by a stroll with the child. This breath from the court was so at variance with her retired home-life and the thoughts that filled her leisure, that she hoped to turn from it to something more real. It seemed to her that Bonaparte was so great there was scarcely room for any unkindness of judgment; but as she had said, she could not have opinions until, at least, she had questioned her husband freely.

"Madame gives me a subject to which I cannot do justice," Alfonte answered with a warmth that was reassuring. "Partly because of my amazement that in times of such upheaval there should be this extraordinary blossoming of art, and partly because the line of its progression is not in my own field, I am not qualified."

"Is it by courtesy that you refuse?"

"Ah, no; I only say what I had believed before I came to France, and now I find it true. Since the Revolution I had heard so much of this rapid development among your painters that I wished to see for myself, and I am not disappointed, David, Gérard, Isabey —their names we know. But besides their canvases and miniatures, by which they are known among us already, I find that they have greatly influenced your society, your customs, your dress, your decorations; the artist element has gotten into them all and made them charming."

"You prove your fitness, signore, in trying to disprove it."

He made a motion of deprecation as he went on—"And I find still further, that your school of artists is chiefly historic, and the time develops them historically; they have had much to do with bringing back the classic outlines which are creeping into your draperies and your coiffures."

"At least, my dear marquise," the countess said, turning to her, "you will admit that if the Consul is cold towards the expression of strong opinions, he knows how to fire the imagination of our artists; for we owe it to him.—Do you not think so, Signore Alfonte ?"

" Your Revolution has done this for France : it has made genius recognizable socially; it has made a place for the new, or at least has made the displacement of existing traditions possible."

" It is one of the growths which the Consul nurses with his extraordinary watchfulness, and to which, by his wise policy, he contributes, even if the times produce it," said the count. "But if Signore Alfonte can say so much for our progress in art, I hope he can also tell us that he has decided to accept the Consul's invitation to make his home in France."

There was a storm of flattering interrogations, while Monsieur de Montal explained with what promise of preferment the invitation had been accompanied.

"It is true your Consul has been most gracious. He has told me he wishes to make his country great in all arts. I appreciate his offers as an honor to my art. But France, with all her splendor and prosperity, is not the home for my noble mistress. I must remain where she would best thrive."

"Then, signore, your words have been but flatteries, after all!" the countess exclaimed in disappointment.

"Not so, madame, I beg of you ; my words are always true. I spoke but of painters, and those only in the field of history or portraiture —not in the field of religion, you will observe, nor of ideality. It is the sort of art that is developed by an epic period: it grows in movement and struggle and change. *My* art demands an atmosphere of repose, and this your Consul, great as he is, cannot create for me !"

CHAPTER SEVENTH.

HE days that followed were full of new experiences for Felix, of which he took in the delight, quite unconscious that he himself played an unusual part in the group which he found so charming. The beautiful boy, so naïve yet so mature, was full of enthusiasm and of quaint ways begotten from the lack of youthful companions and the substitution of heroes, known only through books, for daily friends of living charms and failings: eagerly imitating his elders in every gracious attention of host to guest which this bountiful hospitality was first making known to him, yet escaping self-consciousness and pedantry from his delight in ministering to those about him, he seemed indeed a little prince.

"If the throne of France were to be fitted with a sovereign by vote," the old marquis exclaimed, jocosely, one day, "I believe that boy could unite us all!"

But the child passed harmlessly through the admiration lavished upon him, for his was the unconscious mastery of love, instead of the force of ambition and conscious, unrelenting, self-centred will by which his hero swayed the world.

The development was certainly as charming as it was rare, though in ordinary cases it might not have been a healthy one; nor could it have been produced had life held for Felix the same promise and responsibilities of manhood that it did for other children. But his battle of life was fought for him by those who kept from him all its pain, seeking only his happiness. Guarded, idolized as he was, he was in danger of but one temptation, and selfishness was triumphed over by the ruling motive of his education, the love which also became the central strength of his own character. To this, and to keeping his mind fed on noble thoughts, his parents had trusted for his happiness.

Even the countess found an unexpected satisfaction in noting the deep impression her child was making upon their friends, which partly atoned for the unwonted sense of hurry and confusion of thought produced by this attrition of diverse minds in the hitherto poetic and constant atmosphere of the Château of Val-Maria.

The little fellow was strangely modifying the talk of the circle, for his intense admiration of their First Ruler had been made known to them both by the count and by his own artless and enthusiastic confessions, and not one of them would have pained him by any expression of disloyalty. Thus his eager desire for further information from those who had the great happiness of being continually with the Consul was gratified with every reminiscence that could contribute to the impression

the child had already gained, and as they vied
with each other in culling these bits for Felix,
it was instructive to note how the child's spirit
of love had affected their judgment in anec-
dotes to which a different complexion was
sometimes given in other circles.

He had much to talk over with his marble
friend when left alone with him at night, and
through the door that opened to his mother's
dressing-room she often caught some murmured tones of admiration that seemed to
come from the depths of his heart, and one
evening she distinctly overheard the ardent
words, " Oh, *mon ami—'noblesse oblige;'* and
thou art like a king!"

"Who told you that, my darling?" she
asked, going quickly to him.

"It was Monsieur le Curé, when he was
here to-day," he answered, to her great surprise. "When Monsieur l'Abbé was reading
to us from the *Moniteur* about the Consul's
trip in Belgium ; and how, often, when the
people wanted to make him king, he always
answered that it would be 'unworthy of him

to usurp the authority which must affect the existence of the Republic.'"

The child's training had made such sentiments comprehensible to him, but he repeated the words with pauses, as if he were reciting a lesson imperfectly learned.

"See, *Madonna mia*, here it is; Monsieur l'Abbé gave me the paper. You know I am making my collection for a history I mean to write some day, when I grow up."

She kissed him silently. "But, Felix," after a pause, "what did Monsieur le Curé say?"

"At first he looked as if he did not hear. I thought he did not love our Consul so much as he ought. I thought he was thinking, and perhaps he did not understand. So Monsieur l'Abbé read it once more, very slowly, Monsieur le Curé heard him then, and his eyes grew very bright, and he said, 'My little son, remember that "he that ruleth his spirit is greater than he that taketh a city." It was like a king to refuse the temptation. I am glad the Consul was so noble.'"

Monsieur le Curé had come, as usual, to the

château for *déjeûner* that morning, regardless
of the *grands seigneurs* whom he had declined
to meet at dinner, when the countess had
pressed him to join their party each evening;
for she was proud of the old man, whom she
tenderly loved not alone for his own noble
character, but also for a fancied resemblance
to the grandfather of whom her husband had
so often told her. To this fancy he largely
owed the gentle care of which he never knew
the full measure; the watchfulness over his
wardrobe, which showed a fineness of cloth
and daintiness of cambric and ruffles as un-
suspected by their wearer as they were beyond
his appreciation; the comfort and freshness
and sufficiency of his simple household belongings, at whose unfailing lease of usefulness
and youth he never wondered; the overflow
that was possible from his modest purse or
home, whenever the rare need occurred; the
cheerfulness with which his worthy house-
keeper—his one servant—met all their modest
expenses with the still more modest sum he
placed at her disposal—a sum which bore no

reference to the articles it was intended to purchase, but was simply the remainder from her wages and his disproportionate alms-giving.

If he ever allowed himself a gentle wonder at the time and thought that such matters cost so many of his flock, it passed as quickly as it came—with a sigh for the Marthas cumbered with too much serving—and not without some self-chiding, lest he should be dealing with things he did not understand, for he had a vague consciousness that all "worldly details," as he called everything practical, were beyond his province—not below him, only he was not fitted for them.

If his good Thérèse had ever confessed to the countess's share in the smoothness of his home-ongoings, it might have taken away some of his delight in the dear sense of dependence on the One who had provided that the widow's cruse of oil should not fail, and his gracious friend thought it would be sweeter to him not to know the intervention of any human hand. Thus the little romance had gone on in secret from year to year; and the life which her poetic sympathy thus kept free from earthly frettings often brought its fragrance of peace and holy meditation to enrich the lives of the dwellers in the château.

"I thank you, my daughter," he had said; "I do not change my ways, for I am old, and I have not so many hours left. The evening is my time for going over my 'Legends of the Saints.'"

"Well, then, dear father, you will come to Felix, as usual, for your 'Thursday fête'?"

"Yes, my daughter, I will come," he answered, simply; "I do not change my ways."

So Felix had gone with Monsieur l'Abbé to bring him to the château at the hour which he spent with them each week, and which he called his 'Thursday fête,' from the gentle petting which made it so sweet to him. The countess went forward to receive him, placing him beside her at the table in his special chair, as she was wont to do when they were quite alone. The gentle old pastor made a noble

picture, as simple and dignified among this
brilliant group of courtiers and senators as
when he stood in the midst of his peasant
flock, and as far removed ; for he knew but
little of the things which filled their thoughts.
Nay, further—for these men of the world,
trained to the subtle appreciation of differences,
were more conscious of the aloofness of this
naïve yet imposing figure of peace and duty
well fulfilled, so nearly at the bourn of this
world of change that its changes no longer
either affected or interested him. Little Felix
hovered about him as if he were indeed a
beloved grandfather, and the countess noticed
with content that he carried his atmosphere
with him and was neither confused nor abashed
by the unaccustomed presences in which he
found himself. It was a proof, she thought, as
her glance followed him tenderly, of the power
of a loving life and noble thought to place
those whom the world calls lowly born upon
its highest plane. For the old pastor had
never left his native village, except during the
period of his studies; and with the little

observances of etiquette usual in the classes above his own, the omission of which would have been distinctly observable here, a lifetime of warm intercourse with the inmates of the château had made him so familiar, that their modes of courtesy seemed the natural expression of his own gentle nature.

The talk had turned that morning, before the curé came, on the triumphal procession through Belgium, of which the *Moniteur* gave each day an account more extraordinary than the last; but although the topic had first been introduced by the count, as promising a rest from political discussions that were not always cool, it was soon evident that the event was too important to be without its deductions of still graver import.

For never had a legitimate monarch been received with such a frenzy of enthusiasm— ancient customs wherewith the cities of Belgium had been wont to honor the visits of royalty having been voluntarily offered in testimony of an adulation scarcely befitting a mortal man. On his way thither, at Amiens a crowd of thirty thousand people present their hero with an ovation that savors of fanaticism; some of the most eager unharness his horses and drag the carriage themselves into the city, amidst the *vivas* of the people. It is easy to imagine the tears of joy of the impressionable Josephine; but it was also said that the eyes of the impassive conqueror were humid as he received from the ancient city the tribute of the four white swans which it was its wont to offer only to a sovereign, and the descendants of these royal birds still recite their tale of homage in the garden of the Tuileries.

Everywhere there are illuminations, addresses, throngs gathering from the neighboring towns for one glimpse of this man who sways the world; processions of young maidens clothed in white, bringing offerings of flowers; solemn ceremonials of mighty functionaries, with presentations of keys symbolizing the freedom of cities of which he is already master; grotesque representations of his victories that make the great man smile.

In the midst of all these ovations, Josephine

is more gracious, more winning, more queenly
than ever; but Napoleon does not forget to
weigh and measure, with an accuracy that is
not blinded by all this blaze of glory, the pre-
cise degrees of enthusiasm—one city against
another—and where one is wanting in degree,
he is fertile and politic in resources. "This
people is under the influence of the priests,"
he says to Josephine; "we must spend a long
time in the church before we continue our
route." Hence, in the *Moniteur*, the record of
his profound attention at Mass—his most
gracious words to the archbishop; hence, also,
the acclamations they receive at the grand ball
given by the city, and the allegorical drama
played in the public fête in the great square,
where the rivers of Belgium, conquering the
pride of the Thames, make a peaceful alliance
with the waters of the Seine!

At Antwerp there is no need of an act of
devotion to encourage the enthusiasm of the
jubilant populace; and outside of Brussels a cortége of twelve thousand men is waiting, with
a guard of honor of five hundred of the élite

of the young Belgian nobility, to escort the Consul in safety through the triumphal arch which, modelled after the arch of Titus in Rome, had been erected in his honor, into the streets filled with a joyous crowd, amid the continuous salute of cannon and pealing of chimes and vociferous shouting of "*Vive Bonaparte! vive le grand homme!*" while Josephine follows in a superb carriage presented by the city, and welcomed, as she passes, by a shower of flowers!

The clergy, too, will not be outdone in works of adulation. They stand, in imposing sacerdotal robes, rank upon rank, on the steps of St. Gudule, preceded by the bearer of the Holy Cross, awaiting the victorious Consul : on the steps of this same cathedral that offers him a solemn grand Mass in music on the Sunday that follows, celebrated with extraordinary pomp, where he is received by the clergy and the cross, and conducted by them, under a canopy, to the grand altar. Were ever such honors multiplied upon mortal man? It is no wonder that even a speechless statue, symbolic of its department, after the fashion of France, must flatter him with its legend :

"I bear the name of my department; but thou givest thine to the century !"

The religious aspect and significance of this journey, upon which the Consul had started with the official blessing and prayers of bishops and archbishops, tendered upon his request, had also its keen interest for those who watched the development of France ; and the *Moniteur's* reports of everything bearing upon this question were closely studied. Nor were these priestly mandates lacking in devotion to the great ruler of the nation, "who knew," said the Archbishop of Paris, with a tone which in these days of analysis seems strangely naïve, "that the only way to secure the success of his arms was to interest the God of armies!" But he then proceeds, in a strain of loving earnestness and simplicity which deserved and obtained large results, "He desires that we command your prayers to bring the blessing of heaven upon his righteous undertakings. The love that you bear to your country, my beloved brethren, the gratitude that you owe to a government so mild, so beneficent, so paternal, are a sure guarantee of the zeal with which you will respond to this religious feeling."

Nor was the Archbishop of Rouen behindhand in zeal. "Let us pray God that this man who, under His command, has done so much for the re-establishment of His worship, who proposes to do still more, shall be, like Cyrus, the Christ of Providence. May Providence watch over his life and cover him with His wings, and remove from his august person the dangers found in war for one of such great courage, and those to be feared from envy and detraction for one of such great merit."

"After these benedictory mandates of the archbishops, and the courtly address of Monseigneur of Roquelaure which was reported the other day," said the marquise, looking up from the latest *Moniteur*, "they might have spared themselves the fatigue of preserving this speech of Monsieur le Curé d'Abbeville, for its climax, *en petissant*, seems like a *reductio ad absurdum.* 'Religion, like France, owes to you all that she is; we owe to you all that we are; *I* owe to you all that I am.' Monsieur de Talleyrand did not sift these despatches."

The countess flushed and hastily took a copy of the "Génie du Christianisme" from the table, turning to the dedication. "There is no praise equal to these beautiful words," she said, "and I have heard that the Consul was greatly touched by them. Dear marquise, *must* he not be noble to deserve such eloquence? You remember how the dedication closes: 'Still extend a protecting hand to thirty millions of Christians who pray for you at the foot of the altars you have restored to them.'"

"Bonaparte can be as eloquent as Châteaubriand, I assure you, when the spirit moves him," the marquise answered, with an amiable desire to cover the slight malice of her last remark; "and it may have been Châteaubriand's tribute that moved him to say, not long ago—you know the book only came out last year—'Human pride finds the public it

9*

desires in that ideal world which is called posterity, and he who believes that a hundred years hence a fine poem will recall a great action of his own, has his imagination fired by that idea.'"

At this point Monsieur le Curé had arrived and the countess went forward to receive him, ·but all attempts to draw him into the general conversation proved unavailing. The marquise took a chair beside him, hoping for more success, for his simplicity seemed to her ideal.

"Do you not think with us, Monsieur l'Abbé, that France has at last reached a period of great prosperity ?"

"Pardon me, madame; the title does not belong to me; I am a simple village priest," he said, in tones that were full of courtesy, although they slightly betrayed the peasant accent of his province. "I cannot answer your question, for I know nothing of these things."

"Yet sometimes, out of the turmoil of the world, we come to those who live in quiet for the wisdom of their thoughts; for great thoughts grow in quiet, and priests have swayed the world."

The intended flattery entirely escaped his simplicity.

"I have heard that it has been so," he answered, quietly; "but God has given me, for my duty, only my little parish of Val-Maria, and it has filled my life."

"But, my father," said one of the gentle-men, approaching him with gentle deference, and using the address which he thought would place him most at ease, "surely you are in-terested in what General Bonaparte has done for the Church? He is called its *restorer*."

The old man rose quickly, with a deeper light in his eyes.

"That honor is for no man," he said, glanc-ing around him in grave defiance. "God never ceases to care for His Church!"

Passing through the silenced group, he had reached the terrace windows, when Felix fol-lowed and slipped his soft hand in the curé's withered one. The old man turned suddenly with all his former mildness in his face, look-

ing down at the boy with a smile. "I was
going to seek you in the gardens," he said,
"for our Thursday talk. My daughter, will
you excuse me to your friends? It is the hour
which belongs always to Felix and me."

CHAPTER EIGHTH.

T last the gay company had left, and the château had returned to its former quiet. But there was a great change in Felix, into whose life his new friend Alfonte had poured his own art-wealth. Every morning they had been together for hours in the great library, deep in old folios which brought them into a world of art-treasures, the artist guiding and developing the child's wonderful artistic instincts into a growth which filled his own soul with amazement.

"Never," he declared to the count, "had he found such genius! It was a holy gift!"

But he spoke of it only when they were quite alone, as if it were a coy presence that might not linger if confessed.

" And do not tell the child," he said. " Let us reverence it in silence till I have led him farther on this holy ground. Then he will know it for himself; and the moment of revelation should come within his own soul !"

Often the two friends spoke together of these things, as they strolled up and down the terraces at night, when little Felix was sleeping, filled with new, vague dreams of ecstasy: the beauty that had always ministered so largely to his young and joyous life seemed to whisper to him of shapes that were more tangible, and of a purpose that should make men loftier because he had lived. But it was always beauty whispering, beckoning, eluding—an ideal that he could not reach—with a promise of something divine, beyond his understanding.

One morning he came running to his friend and clasped him close—close—with clinging, passionate arms and cheeks burning with a delicious shame. "I shall be an artist, too !"

he said, in a broken voice. "God told me so last night!"

And the two friends—the lonely artist and the little child whose whole being was wrapped and glorified by love—burst into sobs together. . . .

"Little brother," said Alfonte, at last, "shall we go to the sweet mother and tell her now?"

The child threw back his head, with a clear, ringing laugh, for the mood of quick emotion had passed, leaving him glad-hearted as a bird.

"I cannot tell *Madonna mia* anything," he said. "She knows it always : I think God tells her first."

"Felix, why do you always call her '*Madonna mia*'?"

"I cannot call her anything else," the boy answered, seriously; "there are so many reasons. First, I think it is because I love her so much—the way some one who is very good, like Monsieur le Curé, loves the true Madonna: he tells me about it often when he comes. I love *my* Madonna like that! And

I chose that name for her from all the saints of Monsieur le Curé's legends, because I liked it best."

" And then?——"

" And then her eyes are like the beautiful Madonna of Raffaello that my papa brought home from Dresden. I think I remember that her eyes used to look at me so when I was a little baby like the Holy Child. I don't know if I really *remember* it, because I was so little. I may know it without remembering. I do not always know *how* I know things."

" And then?——" the artist asked again, after a little silence, hesitating to recall the child from his revery, yet fearing to lose some of the sweetness of his thought in its first expansion.

" And then—and then—of course, she would be my Madonna if I were a real knight like those in Froissart's 'Chronicles,' and the olden time my papa tells me about, because she is the sweetest lady in all the world! He says she *can* be my lady now, and lead me on to everything that is holy and noble, as the ladies of the old romance used to do. It is more beautiful to hear my papa talk than even Monsieur le Curé, when he tells me these things ! . . . I do not know my other reasons."

"Felix," Alfonte said, reverently, "it is a very beautiful love. It will make you a noble knight and a great artist. All true artists have been guided by holy loves. Our greatest master, Angelo, was made greater yet by a beautiful and holy lady who taught him the deeper sacredness of art. And the divine Dante—the greatest poet in the world—was made a poet by the dream of a little maiden he had seen but once, and whom he fancied growing more beautiful and saintly every day, until she became his ideal, and the whole world knows the story of this holy love."

"It is a pretty story," said Felix, carelessly; "but it is not like my Madonna ! I want some one to love me, too ; I want some one to love me *very* much !"

"One cannot always have that happiness," Alfonte answered, sadly. "It is possible to

live without the presence of an earthly love to
cheer us, but without an ideal one cannot be
an artist. You remember the face of the
'Laureate,' Felix? I showed it to you the
other day."

"Yes; and I did not like it so well as the
Sanzio's : it made me afraid."

"Yes, but that is only now; later it will
not be so. Felix"—he laid his hand solemnly
on the radiant young head—"art will ask
more and more of us as time passes, and we
must not be afraid of her sublimity. She
makes men lonely, for they must meditate in
solitude, or they cannot hear her speak. She
must be a great love; she must be a religious
passion; she must make men loftier; she must
lift them up to heaven itself. Art is the echo
of the voice of God within us and about us,
and she is divine!"

The child looked at him with great shining
eyes.

"Dear master," he said, very softly and
slowly, as if pledging himself to the noble
creed, "I know it ! and now"—with the quick

change of mood vibrating, bird-like, through his tones and his joyous, rhythmic motions— "I must go to *Madonna mia ;* so many things have happened since she kissed me this morning !"

Oh, the long delight of the time that followed, when the boy was led, step by step, by his artist friend to a comprehension—beyond his years, and possible only to true genius— of the science and technique that were needed at the very threshold of this glorious Temple of Art which he aspired to enter as a disciple. The resources of the château had offered much for their study, and the exhaustless stores of the master's mind had endued its treasures with a living interest they had never before possessed, as they studied in gallery, chapel, or library, or dwelt on old myths and classic stories among the marble images on the terrace.

Meanwhile a studio had been prepared for Alfonte's group, his " master-work of Mother-Love," as even then he dared to name it, before he had touched his model—so sure had

he felt from the beginning of his inspiration ;
nor were they satisfied with the rude studio
first intended when the group had been dis-
cussed, for was it not to belong to Felix? and
after the words Alfonte had spoken, must they
not do all that was possible to aid in the development of their child's wondrous gift? So
a vast room, connecting with Felix's chamber,
and opening directly back of it upon a large
upper terrace or gallery, was dismantled of its
guest-chamber furnishings and completely re-
fitted as Alfonte directed; and here he was
bidden to order everything as he would have
it for a model studio. Great boxes came from
Florence and Rome, with treasures, rich in
educational value, that were to belong to
Felix, many of them gifts from Alfonte's own
store ; there were trained assistants from his
studio in Florence, with implements and artists'
belongings ; and finally all was complete. The
studio was an artist's realization, with draperies and bits of color against which the carefully-
selected antique casts were outlined ; with
cosey spots inviting to meditation by their rugs

and cushions and quaint deep chairs, here and there, among the ample rougher spaces that permitted work. But when all was finished, it was Felix who thought of the special couch and easy-chair, the little table for her work or book, and the great vases of growing plants for mamma's own corner, and who led her to it as if she had been a queen, with a beautiful, grave, and courtly grace; and who, the moment she was established there, danced about with the most childish and vehement expressions of delight, quite inappropriate to the master of such a studio. Mamma, too, first arrayed him in the long white linen tunic she had had prepared to slip over his velvet suit, and fitted his crimson cap over his bright hair, with an air of robing him for some great initiation ceremony. And here the little acolyte began his apprenticeship, while Alfonte, who had replaced his brilliant court-dress with a loose gray studio tunic and dark-green velvet cap, gave himself up to the joy of his creation; and the countess worked or read on her low couch, or talked with the count, who, in the first days of this great new interest, was often with them.

An immense old-fashioned dormer-window, that was in fact a projecting gable, and had always been used as a dressing-room, opened from one end of this great chamber, and this had been remodelled with added lights in the roof, and a system of easy mechanism, by which these and the original lower lights could be adjusted, had been provided; stone columns had been carried down to the lower terrace, affording an ample support; and the floor of this space, which was in all respects much rougher than the rest of the apartment, had been plainly tiled to receive the drippings from the modeller's work; and here rose the first rude semblance of the group upon which Alfonte labored with a zeal that was infectious.

"Take something you know thoroughly for your first attempt," the master said, as he left the boy dreamily pondering over the first mass of clay he was to shape quite alone.

His mother smiled at him from her distant corner, and the happy thought that came with the smile was soon pulsating through his eager finger-tips, and with a deft manipulation of the little wooden spaddles that astonished the assistant who was bringing water and clay for the master. Alfonte, who had been wholly absorbed in indicating his attitudes and massing his draperies, folded him closely in his arms when Felix showed him the first offering of his *culte*, for so perfectly had he delineated his mother's hand that it could not be mistaken.

" It is my guiding hand," he said, his sweet face all aglow.

There were often days when the countess or her child, or both, would be asked to pose, and the work would proceed with enthusiasm; then there would be others when Alfonte would see no one but Felix, sending away his assistant, and begging that no other footsteps might come near his studio ; he would even send the boy away, with a command that he should not return unless he were summoned; for there were times when the passion of his creation led him through stormy places, and he needed to be alone to work out his inspiration.

And again there were periods of suspension in which nothing of his thought could be evolved, mornings in which work was done and undone in the pliant clay ; and others when he would not enter the studio at all, except for Felix.

And once, when Alfonte, with a face that glowed like a vision, had bolted himself in alone with Felix, showing him by an imperious gesture that he must not speak, the child, breathless and awe-stricken, had watched the quick strokes with a swelling pity in his loving, sympathetic soul, for on his dear master's face the light of inspiration was changing to a passion of pain ; but before his little, pleading hands could arrest the motion, Alfonte, in a frenzy of disappointment, had thrust his spaddle deep into the clay, undoing not only the troubled work of the morning, but much that had been wrought with careful and responsive touch, and seizing the child's hand with a grasp so passionate that he instinctively shrank from it, though his whole soul yearned to comfort his beloved master, Alfonte strode out with steps so quick and uneven that Felix could scarcely keep pace with them as he ran by his side.

Yet the little hand was not too tightly prisoned to convey a faint caress, and presently Alfonte's grasp relaxed as he felt it struggling within his own, and looking down with a tenderness the deeper for his momentary forgetfulness, he saw that Felix was trying to repress a sigh of fatigue.

"It was because I loved you that I brought you!" he cried, as he gathered the little fellow close in his arms as a mother might have done, and pressed the fresh cheek passionately against his own. "I love you so much that I could not do without you, and yet I have hurt you, my Felix! But you cannot know, my child—you cannot know!—This morning, when I woke, and all through the night, I had been longing for the day, for I heard my art calling to me, urging me on, so that I felt I could not fail her! But art was born in me too late, my Felix. I did not grow and live in her life through a beautiful childhood, as thou art doing. God has filled my soul full of her passion, but my hands were late in training to her cunning, and sometimes I cannot speak my thought.   Live close to art; think only this one thought, of God and Art!"

"And Love," said Felix, very softly, and nestling closer.

"Ay. God and Love and Art are one; only God and Love can create Art."

And so, through many months, the work grew with uneven steps of progress, while the greater work of the developing of an artist grew daily with rapid pace that never turned backward, and in this unfolding Alfonte's interest never flagged.

One day when they were alone together, Alfonte said, with great emotion, "Once I thought but of my work: I dreamed that I lived for that! Now, my child, I live for yours!"

But there came a day when the exquisite model was completed—when the artist, with hands that feared to add another touch, stood, battling with his disappointment, before his realization, questioning if he had uttered all his thought, and how much more that marble "resurrection" which is the sculptor's hope should emphasize its spirituality.

But the count was speechless from emotion, and Felix was in a turmoil of delight.

"My hope was far beyond this—far beyond," Alfonte said later, as they all gathered about his group. "But there are lines that are too subtle for the clay. I do not know—the transparency of the marble has promise in it, and it shall be begun at once, while my conception is still vivid. I will write to-night to Carrara to reserve the first choice for me; and when the casting is finished, I will go at once.

"And, my friend, Felix must go with me. I shall take him to Florence and to Rome; it is needful for him to get into an atmosphere of art. He must know the immortal Angelo by his works. He must study now from the divinest of our masters, for I alone might dwarf his gift."

After that, while he remained at Val-Maria, he was always watching the mother and child whenever they were together.

"There is always something beyond our art," he confessed to the count, "in an ideal human life; a suggestion of the infinite which artists may seize but not convey. And this group which I have dreamed of so long—so long—the veriest sublimity of human love—I fear it has a thought of too much passion to be wrought in marble. I have come so near to my ideal only to be saddened by art's limitations and my own."

In vain his friend sought to reassure him. "It is the mothers only who are artists with a hope," Alfonte said; "for they are the sculptors of deathless souls!"

Were they right in feeling that a new radiance had crept into their child's life? the father and mother asked each other, mutely, as they followed the eager movements of the young priest of art, in his fair white garments of consecration, and wondered at the forms of beauty that responded to his magic touch. Was it only that his artist soul was satisfied to create? or did the wondrous glow of cheek and lip, the strange, glad fire that had deepened in his eyes, the richer flow of life that rounded each swaying motion, echoing the fulness of his happiness as words utter the thoughts of others—did these indeed indicate a new glow of physical life for their beloved one?

"My wife," the count said at length, in answer to her mute, pathetic inquiry, "shall we have the courage *not* to ask? Men know so little—even those who think they know!"

"But, Louis, if they were to tell us, our fear might end."

"Beloved, think how their words have blighted the joy of all these beautiful years! God's ways are more merciful than man's. Let us not seek to know."

"But, Louis," she persisted, piteously, yet relentless to herself, in the strength and weakness of her great love, "do *you* not think it may be fuller life?"

She looked up beseechingly in his face: it was full of a solemn light of peace—the look of one who has struggled and conquered.

He held her close for a moment, without speaking. "God help you, my darling," he said; "it *is* fuller life. Let us be grateful for His gifts. But, sweet mother of our child, do you remember how we pledged each other to make his life the happiest that had ever gladdened God's earth? And has not the answer come most wondrously—in a life so rich—as if the joy of years were lived in each of its full hours? He radiates joy like the sunlight!"

"You mean it is too much? Louis, it makes you afraid?"

"No, darling, not afraid, for God has sent it, and it must be well. But it is very wonderful; and sometimes, when I remember that a thousand years in His sight are but as a moment, and a moment may mean His fulness of time, I think we may not measure human life with human measures."

They were silent for a while, and she felt the quiet of the night, or the holier quiet of his speech, steal into her soul like balm. "I have come to understand the sweetness *of not knowing*," he said at length, "when knowledge rests with One who is all love!"

"You comfort me, dear Louis."

"Let me do more than that," he said, very earnestly, "as gladness is higher than comfort! I stand in awe before my own little child, for a power has awaked within him that is beyond our guiding, and we must give it sway. But shall we not also yield to his mission? For I trust we live in the knowledge and faith of God, but Felix seems wholly to outbreathe the Eternal Love and Joy!"

CHAPTER NINTH.

IT was perhaps more difficult in the last days of the Consulate and the first of the Empire for a Frenchman to analyze the state of the mind of France in regard to its government, than it is for us, nearly a century later, to determine how it was then regarded. For a man like Montal, feeling that he ought to devote his talents to the immense problems of his time, the struggle was a great one; for he would not submit to bow to mere intellectual force, however splendid, unless he felt that force to be ruled by principle, and the man who swayed the Empire and its great dependencies pos-

sessed an inscrutable personality that was never
fully revealed to friend or foe.

If Napoleon had astonished the world by the
soldier-craft which had so increased the do-
minion of France, he was yet more wonderful
in his comprehensive statesmanship, seeing all
things at once with those keen eyes under the
narrowed lids, and dropping no thread of the
vast machinery he had set in motion, yet keeping one hand always free for the tracing of
new plans and charts in the sleepless midnight
hours; for so abnormally was he constituted
that from time also he could command double
service, three hours sufficing for his nightly
sleep and fifteen minutes for his most cere-
monious meal!

If the world knew him on one side only, it
would have called him great; but he was so
many-sided that he became incomprehensible.

We find ourselves touched by the sight of
the Emperor reviewing his troops with one of
Josephine's grandchildren in his arms—the one
whom he had chosen for his heir: he was fond
of children and charming to them; and at

times in the family circle he was genial, un-
bending, interested in trifles, showing something of the fondness of ordinary men; but
these were mild interludes: the glory of
France was always supreme, and to this everything must be sacrificed. But he had expanded
in this forcing atmosphere of his own success
with an unprecedented bloom ; the *gaucheries*
of his first entrée into circles that had looked
upon him askance were no longer remembered ; everywhere he dominated.

In the first days of the Consulate he used
more largely the gifts of charming with which
he was endowed, winning men rather by their
hearts than forcing their assent to his empire ;
and while he was still climbing, he relied upon
those who were competent in fields unknown
to him, leading them by honors and munificence to do their best for France.

"It is strange," thought Montal, "that one
who so newly wears the purple can grasp these
vast interests and direct their minutest details ;
but it is not strange that the world should bow
to such dominance, for he puts forth every

energy to achieve it." For the statesman and aristocrat found himself ceaselessly occupied with this extraordinary personality and with France, as separate entities, not necessarily opposed, neither necessarily one, as they seemed to others, and yet together composing an inscrutable problem; and for a time circumstances strangely favored his investigations, bringing him, almost against his will, into a closer intimacy with the circle in power than he would have chosen ; for he was early aware that he was being rather weighed than consulted, when there had been occasional conversations of some length between Bonaparte and himself, where the apparent deference of the First Consul had filled the hearts of those who craved such favor with thoughts that were not gracious. Montal's attendance had been often required in matters of importance, and he had had many opportunities, in this close contact which he had not sought, for the study which fascinated him the more because he was conscious that in the presence of this conqueror of wills his own inner self was not dominated ;

he also could weigh and judge, if a little indignant with himself at a suspicious temper
which he felt to be almost at variance with
knightly grace.

Thus he knew that in the hours that others
give to sleep, Napoleon was shaping his great
schemes in his wonderful brain ; in times of
war busy with chart and pencil planning the
campaign, choosing the lines of march from a
thorough knowledge of the country laboriously
gained, or studying, as his army marched forward, the needs of conquered provinces or
neglected cities ; decreeing buildings, or roads,
or vast border works, or planning new con-
stitutions with equal ease and judgment. In
times of peace taking thought for the arts
and sciences and letters, conferring honors to
tempt to their pursuit, and inviting artists from
other lands to make their home in France.

If there were too great a rush of leisure in
these days and nights, there was the *Code
Napoléon*, raised stone by stone, little by little,
into the masterly monument the world has
received !

The *Moniteur* was his organ; and in its columns, carefully revised on their literary side by his secretaries, to guard against the defects of his speech, appeared the opinions he thought it wisest for his people to hold upon all matters of the government—views he wished to present of questions yet to be decided; accounts that seemed to him most politic, of the battles fought, accounts often written in his own hand, illegible and badly spelled, hot from the battle-field—sometimes translating an actual defeat by the more gracious word of "victory," and choosing his own terms of self-laudation, as in this authentic report of a phrase dictated by the Emperor in a war-bulletin: "The panegyric of the army may be pronounced in two words, 'It was worthy of its leader.'"

Yet, although the officers often murmured loudly at the false reports returned, which stripped some of their honors and conferred laurels where they were not due, the wonderful strategic power of their great general, his bravery, his magnetism, his way of putting

_i

young men in places where they might distinguish themselves; the gift of an unequalled memory for faces and names and deeds that are dear to the soldier's heart, his power of associating these deeds with the face, leading him to recall them aloud whenever he was brought face to face with a decorated man of the ranks, made him deservedly an idol with his army. This power, like so many of his qualities, came largely from his genius for work, for Josephine tells us that when he was a young officer he committed to memory, each night, the names and deeds on the honor-roll of his command, continuing the habit of repeating these lists aloud until he feel asleep.

The only possible way of accounting for some visible incongruities in a character that seemed so largely under its own control was that in all that concerned the government he felt himself to be the State; here he was always judicial, inflexible, unmoved by any suspicion of feeling, ungoverned by any principle except that of the glory of the country he ruled; and his family, to its remotest branches, must centre in himself and live for this sole end. Hard as it is to offer such an estimate of any human being, when we remember the littleness of man without his noblest attribute, it seems as if Napoleon, having reached the imperial throne, became devoid of pure affections; as if all that appeared like evidences of such emotion were simply simulated from policy, so entirely were all who depended upon him ignored when their wishes or happiness crossed, at any angle, his vision of the Apotheosis of Self.

This estimate of Napoleon, which Montal reached very slowly and after great perplexity, he hesitated to acknowledge by an open defection from his post, lest he should be recording an unfair judgment; not realizing that a step which meant so much for him was of no feather's weight in that stately legislative body which no longer echoed any but the imperial will. But his vehement protestations against the abuse of the rights of the people had ceased; one voice was powerless; and while his sense of right had not changed, he was dazed and bewildered by the wonderful personality which imposed upon such a body of men, that seemed equal to directing all things, and had crowned France with an unequalled prosperity.

Thus he watched eagerly and silently, wondering at his own lack of enthusiasm when thickening honors were voted — a Roman Triumph, an Imperial Column, the writing of the conqueror's words in deathless marble; when the Pope himself deigned to respond to the summons for the Imperial Coronation, and the whole nation breathed out incense.

Should he still hold his own views of right above those of all the world? Montal asked himself. How was it possible that he alone should have light? he alone, while appreciating this enormous talent, feel such terrible distrust? Yet he could not act against his own inner light, however feeble or erring; and this very loyalty to his own convictions, against the judgment of a nation, constituted in his fair mind a plea for the man in whom he no longer believed. For Napoleon, too, he told himself, might be honestly living according to his light;

he might honestly believe himself created to replace the ancient dynasty, by whatever means; for had ever man received more overwhelming recognition of his power, more surprising responses to his schemes? The confusion was paralyzing, and Montal at length felt that he must resign his post, while he still asked himself, "What have I done for France, that I may venture to censure this man who has done so much?"

It was a curious sight, this Parisian throng, whose study had so attracted the young senator-philosopher as he reviewed the changing drama of the Convention and Consulate and Empire. Motley, contented—singing snatches of the various songs composed for the superb fêtes to which they were treated in these days—very republican it was in theory, while unconsciously subservient to the slightest indication of the will of its dictator. People and army were hand-in-hand, for was it not the army who had made France? And when the army's chief had been formally installed in the Palais du Gouvernement—the royal home of the ancient, overturned kings of France—what a triumph for democracy, who thronged the ways and filled the air with their exultations, as the procession passed the hedge of the Consular Guard, from the Place du Carrousel to the door of the palace, in sight of that inscription written with red revolutionary fingers on the palace wall. "The 10th of August, 1792, royalty was abolished in France, never to be revived!"

Upon the palace walls, too, was graven in letters of gold the word "République:" it gleamed a glorious safeguard in the eyes of the happy people, as Napoleon passed under the portal of the Tuileries; but they did not hear his words to Josephine, as the days wore on, "I leave it there as one writes the name on a picture it is hard to recognize!"

How should the people fear for their rights when the very hacks that followed in that strange procession were the confiscated coaches of the crushed nobility, shabby and misused, with plebeian numbers pasted over their humiliated crests, their owners—*émigrés*—stealing back into France under feigned names, to plead for the restoration of their rights?

Surely the people need not fear with a chief who pledged them thus loyally at the grand banquet of the national fête: " To the 14th of July and the French people—our Sovereign !" Had they not listened to the strong republican speech of Carnot, the Minister of War, in the Temple of Mars, on the anniversary of the founding of the Republic?

And could they forget the eloquent words of the Minister of the Interior, Lucien Bonaparte, at the fête générale de la paix : " O France ! Republic cemented by the blood of heroes and of victories, may Liberty—so much the more precious because she has cost so dear—and Peace, the repairer of every ill, ever remain your tutelary deities !"

And were not these the words of one who had vowed to pierce the heart of his own brother with his sword, if ever that brother should prove false to the liberties of France?

But now, as Montal paced the streets of Paris —how changed from the days of the Directory!

—filled with a brilliant throng and echoing with the *vivas* of the coronation fête, he was reasoning against his reason, to quiet his discontent. The very names had been changed to record the victories and prosperity of the times. The Place de la Concorde was a souvenir of the glorious fête de la paix générale, that phœnix which had risen from the ashes of the 18th Brumaire, the wings brilliantly feathered with the treaties of peace with England, La Porte, Tunis, Algiers, Bavaria, and Russia ! And a brother of the Consul held the pen with which these negotiations were signed.

Still pacing this storied square, the ancient Place de la Révolution, through which, ever and anon, carriages passed him bearing ancient crests, while the old faces looked out at the windows to direct the footmen who wore the ancient familiar liveries, or to exchange greeting with occupants of other carriages wearing the liveries and crests of new titles of the Empire, Montal remembered that it was not alone of the people that Napoleon had declared "Luxury and glory have never failed to turn the

heads of the French!" While Consul he had
discovered that the *noblesse* also would come
and shine for him, if his court but offered
sufficient glitter to reflect their brilliancy; and
with slow steps, befitting their dignity, the
proud habitués of the salon of Josephine on
the rez-de-chaussée of the Tuileries—*émigrés*,
Royalists and representatives of the old *régime*,
who had always felt themselves at home in her
gentle and gracious presence—had overcome
their prejudices, and mounted the stairs that
led to the reception-rooms of the First Consul.

Memories of other fêtes came to Montal as
he stood pondering, each one emphasizing some
great advance in restoration, pacification, ac-
quisition, or reform—the words seemed almost
synonymous to him in his confusion and dis-
quiet, and in his vexation at his own irritabil-
ity in the face of such radiant prosperity. The
coming of the Papal legate, bringing the *Concordat,* on the 15th of July, 1801; the addresses
of congratulation from all sides that the Consul
had shared with the Senate. Why could he
not rejoice more whole-heartedly in the present

position of the Church ?   Was not this alone
sufficient to win the unswerving fealty of every
son of the Church to the restorer of its liberties ?   It had been no easy matter for the great
chief of the army to secure that first brilliant
celebration of Mass at Notre-Dame, on Easter
Day, 1802 ; and the murmurings and scoffs of
the officers had not been uttered *sotto voce ;*
for they did not profess to abandon the license
of the Revolution for a loftier faith.   Yet Montal could not disabuse himself of the ungener-
ous thought that this restitution also was the
triumphant result of policy, entirely divorced
from any true religious feeling, and with a
man so staunch and uncompromising as the
count this effectually chilled all response.   He
could stand unmoved, except by a feeling akin
to indignation, before the windows of the
book-stores which displayed an allegorical
engraving representing the "Triumph of religion in France over revolutionary atheism,
with the Cross of Christ upheld by the sword
of Bonaparte."

There was always a little group before these

windows, chiefly in caps and blouses, with often a priest to explain the sentence that was written underneath: "The 28th Germinal of the French Republic, Easter Day, by the triumphant arm of Napoleon Bonaparte, First Consul of France, religion arose from the abyss where she had been plunged by the godless and atheists." And a little judicious commotion was kept up by the police before these book-stalls with their oft-repeated "*Allons, messieurs;* move on, if you please. A little more space!" in tones sufficiently insistent to attract the oncoming blouses and caps, who also paused to learn the lesson set them and to hear echoed from mouth to mouth how the Archbishop of Paris said Mass every Sunday at the Tuileries; and how the Sunday was always a holiday now in the official bureaus, "as it used to be before the Revolution."

"*Allons, messieurs;* move on!" for the word had a dangerous ring that neutralized the loyalty of the sentiment, and the police were trained to vigilance.

"Every one is trained to vigilance!" Montal mused. "Is this man who calls himself our Emperor, superhuman—a monarch of souls?"

Thence he glided easily into thoughts of the Roman Empire, the deification of the Emperor arising as a natural consequence of the Roman's strict obedience to will, whence the chief ruler became the living symbol of law, and the people acknowledged that he held the position by divine right. Yet the Romans believed that the laws which they obeyed with such unquestioning devotion had been framed by their human law-giver through a divine inspiration : it was a thought that might command the allegiance of strong men, through which their government became the highest earthly expression of their religion. "It is in this effete Roman sense of the word," Montal thought, bitterly, "that our Emperor would have France regard religion in our modern day —as obligation, or binding power, to an absolute despot! He looks on war, too, with the Roman mind, as a religious act ; hence these thickening complications with England and this growing recklessness of life!" Some familiar words of Virgil glided into his scholarly mind —"Thy work, O Roman! is to rule the nations; these be thine arts: to impose the conditions of the world's peace, to show mercy to the fallen, and to crush the proud," and as he mused on the points of similarity between the Napoleonic and the Roman ideal, he felt that as a pagan, owning no will higher than his own, Napoleon would indeed have been very great.

This, then, gave him a hint of the lacking element.

Montal was convinced that the French people by their blind adulation were responsible for the form which the government had now assumed, and which they were henceforth powerless to direct, having voluntarily yielded up their liberties. He had seen much of Bonaparte in the early days of the Republic, and he was strongly inclined to the belief that at that time he was a loyal supporter of republican principles, intending faithfully to guard the liberties of the people, possibly to aid in the restoration of a constitutional monarchy, to be represented by a prince of the House of Bourbon. He had often spoken of this belief with Carnot, who confirmed him in it; and with Joseph Bonaparte, who had absolute faith in the republican principles of his brother; even with Josephine, who was not only a friend of the Royalists, but an open espouser of their cause, and a firm believer in the restoration by her husband's hand.

At this time it had been evident that Napoleon's feeling for Josephine was real, and deep enough to be the noblest influence of his life— deep enough to have deepened to save him; while now, at the period of the coronation, the condition of court morality was one of the terrible symptoms to which Montal could no longer blind himself.

Yet there were gracious memories of a life at Malmaison, poetic and charming, when Bonaparte had been a genial and delightful host, seemingly unspoiled by the greed of power,—his sterner qualities softened by his love for poetry, his delight in sounds that were soft and sweet, in music, in church-bells, in the human voice, his half-confessions of faith in old superstitions and traditions which moved him still on the side of romance, though his reason had grown away from them—a remembrance of early faith still reverent, though not dominant. It seemed more than probable that there had been an early turning-point in the life of the boy who had been from his childhood poetic and dreamy, when he chose his life of action instead of that of a poet or dreamer, in which some critics think he would have been very great—so vivid and far-reaching was his imagination, and so indomitable was he in whatever he elected to accomplish.

While his thoughts were absorbed by this master-figure of his century, Montal found himself often going back to this fancied turning-point with a strange fascination, seeking out all the noble attributes of this man's nature, watching their gradual development until they had mastered his weaknesses, realizing his life dominated by the religious principle which was to him an essential of greatness. What might not such a man have accomplished for the good of the world !

But there was no one with whom he could share this dream, which always ended in a great wave of pity for the possible greatness that had been surrendered to reach this height of earthly glory. It was the dream of a poet, a statesman, and a religious enthusiast—the conception of one who realized the nobility of these callings and the divine possibilities of man's nature in the acknowledged strength of God.

Perhaps, in those early days of the Consulate, Napoleon's character had really touched its height; perhaps he was then truly fired with a patriotic love for France, feeling himself extraordinarily endowed for its rescue. But watching keenly, it was easy to trace the growth of absolutism in the schemes of the chief of the Republic, gradually gaining empire until his thought had framed a government as arbitrary as that of imperial Rome, with a system of religion and of feudal accessories, studied from the time of Charlemagne, that tended greatly to increase the central power.

Perhaps it might have been well for the lustre of Napoleon if the extension of the Consulate to the ten years first offered him had been the term of the Senate's homage, instead of that quick submission of " Consulate for life," so closely followed with imperial honors and rights of imperial succession. It would surely have been better for the liberties of France ; for since the nation had placed him on its highest pinnacle, and could offer him nothing more, although he still felt that the destiny of the nation was indissolubly connected with his own, it was, even to himself, an imperceptible change to seek whatever tended to his own glory as best for France, while, as by some subtle fallacy of mathematical progression, the point of passing could not be distinguished.

Neither Montal nor Carnot had been of those who voted to change the Republic to an Empire, and when the senators dashed from the Chamber to their carriages, to be the first to carry the news to St. Cloud and make their obeisance to the new Cæsar, Montal had gone sadly to the library of Carnot and confessed to him, in deep humiliation, that his faith in Napoleon was gone, and his resignation must follow.

Carnot listened with an uncompromising silence that chafed the younger man almost unbearably, for although he had not unfolded the beautiful dream which his generous soul had wrought from his early hopes of Napoleon, he had spoken hotly of the conclusion reached through strong travail of spirit; for it was a bitter thing to him to be forced to abandon all part in public life because he had lost his faith in the man who had usurped the supreme power over the country and the institutions that he revered.

Montal had not expected full sympathy, but he had looked for some comprehension of his trial. "Either I am wrong," he cried out, desperately, "or France is in great danger!"

But the man who had signed the death-warrant of Louis XVI. could answer him without emotion, as, from the Place de la Bastille up to the royal palace of the Tuileries, and

down through the ancient Place de la Révolution, the rejoicing of the fickle city flashed
forth in long lines of illumination over the
death of the Republic and the birth of the
Empire.

CHAPTER TENTH.

I N the first loneliness of the surrender of his ideal, Montal had felt too weak to bear the vast emptiness of Paris ; its atmosphere, shot through and through with splendor, chilled and oppressed him ; he could find no satisfaction even in the reforms which he knew to be good *per se*, for his whole nature was in a state of fierce revolt, and he felt that he could not breathe freely until he was again surrounded by the love and truth of his home-life in Val-Maria ; and thither he went at once, to reflect upon the action he should take.

When he reached the bridge between the château and the village street, he stopped before the quaint shrine, descending from his travelling-carriage, as if he would pay homage to the rude, time-scarred image; and standing there reverently for a moment with uncovered head, he was pleased to see that a few fresh field-flowers lay at the feet of this Madonna Val-Maria. In the little village, at least, there were still those who kept to the simple faith of the olden days, he said to himself with a sigh of relief, as he passionately renewed the vow with which he had entered so hopefully upon his young manhood, to struggle for right and truth and for justice towards the classes who could not plead for themselves—the vow of every true knight of Montal. He would still use his birthright of nobility and his strength as a man, independent of all parties, to wield whatever influence God had given him. In Paris, if it seemed best, when he had regained his composure, or even here, in his own province, he might still labor with his pen, for words of truth have outlived empires, and God only asks of each human soul its own possible best; He, the Merciful, does not weigh the weakness of one against the power of another, and find the weak one wanting.

The very sight of this peaceful home, sleeping in the moonlight, and the little village calmly trusting to the guardianship of the time-defaced Madonna, who was still clothed with the graceful strength of the old tradition, had revived his heart. He, the master of the château, would not fail them! and the sense of the duty that depended upon him, small as it would have seemed to the legislators he had left, came upon him with a new sweetness; and he could meet his wife more calmly than he had dreamed possible in the great hall of the château, whose quaint carved rafters of feudal days, enriched with mottoes and quarterings of successive generations, seemed to offer him an unlooked-for support, an assurance that those who had lived before him in the long line of noble ancestry looked to him, at this crisis, to be worthy of an honorable past. And for one of the count's strong beliefs the help was real rather than visionary.

Later there was a long, quiet talk, wearing

into the morning, in which Montal revealed his bitter disappointment to his wife, not hiding his fears for France; for between these two everything was shared.

" And Felix?" she asked, when their discussion of the case was finished.

" Ah, Felix?" he questioned, in quick alarm.

"Dear Louis, you know how he worships the Emperor; you know it would break his heart to tell him the truth!"

He looked at her, smiling, from his sense of relief. "Ah, well," he said. "Do you remember Pilate's question? We need tell Felix nothing. It is well indeed that some of us may keep our beautiful faiths."

Finally, Montal, feeling himself refreshed and invigorated by the true and tranquil home-life of Val-Maria, had again returned to Paris, deciding for a little longer to hold his post and watch if by any means he might yet serve France with speech or vote within the Senate.

Carnot received him without surprise or comment, and they took their seats together. But the fire had died out of Montal's utterances;

he scarcely knew himself when he stood up, single-handed and sore at heart, to deliver some argument which he had wrought out fiercely, in solitary vigils in the Hôtel Montal, meaning by his eloquence to carry the House upon some point that concerned the liberties of the people. But the words that had first been flung like hot lead into the cold bath of this unsympathetic atmosphere, soon dropped brokenly, cooling before they reached the ears of a body scarcely tolerant of any interruptions in offering their assent to a measure that had been proposed by the Emperor. The result was always the same, and his courage was well-nigh spent, for it was a thankless task to represent the opposition unsupported. Carnot said nothing, but was unapproachable, and invited him to no more conferences in his study; Monsieur de Rémusat bestowed a kindly word of caution; and Monsieur de Talleyrand reminded him, with his admirable tact, that a courtier deals rather with success than theories, however praiseworthy.

Thus, in despondence and mental isolation,

he sat in solitary judgment upon the brilliant events that were passing around him, exchanging a rare confidence with Madame de Rémusat, who, if not of his opinion, once showed herself willing to think for herself by confessing, "The situation is greatly changed; so are men's minds."

This was in 1805, and the Emperor's life now offered an unbroken succession of pomps and triumphs. In May he assumed, in response to the petition of the Italian republic, conveyed through a deputation from Milan, the Iron Crown of Italy, the Senate naturally approving, with addresses of commendation; for surely this was a legitimate increase of the national prestige, since, seated on his throne, the Emperor had listened to the request of the Council that he would graciously consent to reign over the Ultramontane republic also. "Our present government," said the vice-president, "cannot continue, because it throws us behind the age in which we live. Constitutional monarchy is everywhere indicated by the finger of progress."

The pomp of the ceremonial and the ring of the antique formula, " Il cielo me la diède, guai à chi la toccherà," caused new rejoicing among the people ; but Montal was of the few who questioned the policy of the investiture of the Iron Crown, fearing that war with Austria might result, as he recalled with anxiety the words Napoleon had spoken of that other diadem he wore with such superb assurance : "I found the crown of France lying on the ground, and I picked it up on the point of my sword !" In fact, the Austrian discontent was at that moment being skilfully fanned into life by the hatred of England, and preparations for war were going on in secret, while there was no open rupture between France and Austria.

Early in June, when the coronation fête was scarcely ended, the Doge of Venice reached Milan with a fresh sprig of laurel for the con-queror's crown, imploring that his republic might form part of the Empire. It is difficult to say whether this presentation had been previously commanded, but it added a distinct note to the chorus of jubilee, although but a few months before the voice of the dictator of Europe had proclaimed without disguise, " The dynasty of Naples has ceased to reign. Its existence is incompatible with the repose of Europe and the dignity of my crown !"

Meanwhile this extraordinary prosperity continued without rebate, at home and abroad, at the dawning of the year 1806, when Regnault de St. Jean d'Angely, the Councillor of State, declared in a remarkable report which seemed to echo the feeling of the nation, "France has nothing to ask from heaven but that the sun may continue to shine, the rain to fall on our fields, and the earth to render the seed fruitful." But late in March an important session of the Senate gave rise to something akin to discussion, for which Montal prepared himself with a return of his old ardor and not a little hope, for the Emperor had communicated a long list of decrees that would importantly affect the welfare of Europe.

But the statesman's insight, however cogently reasoned, fell flat upon the specious speech of Cambacérès: "You will receive with gratitude these fresh proofs of the Emperor's confidence in the Senate and his love for the people, and hasten, in conformity with his Majesty's intention, to inscribe them on your registers."

The supplies were immediately voted as desired, all the proposed measures were approved, and the new titles were created ; again addresses of compliment were carried in the Senate and published in the *Moniteur*, and later there were glowing accounts of the triumphal entrées of these princes without pedigrees into the principalities they were henceforth to rule ; but already an undertone of disbelief was beginning to whisper that truth was not an essential ingredient of the tidbits of "current opinion" that were served out daily to the French people.

Montal, utterly disheartened, gave up his seat and withdrew altogether from public life, feeling that he no longer cared to utter opinions so at variance with the judgment and action of the most important men of his time, while he was yet conscientiously unable to conform to the popular belief of infallibility which, to the prejudiced eyes of a loyal son of the Church, seemed to have moved its centre from Pope to monarch with the easy grace that made such revolutions a matter of course in these strange times.

He would have liked to forget the government, if he might; he longed to get himself out of the blaze of this mastering personality which, like too intense a sunlight, seemed to dazzle the world into blindness. He would have liked to persuade himself that, without disloyalty to himself or to his nation, he might abandon the perplexing problems with which he had so vainly striven, and yield himself freely to the rest of body and spirit which he now sought in Val-Maria.

But even in this tranquil spot, which charmed him like a bit of old-time romance when he first returned to it wearied with the strain of his unsatisfying political life, he soon found that the shadow of the glory of the mastering personality, if less dominant, had penetrated also.

In his first visit to Monsieur Simon, he found the old curé in poignant distress over a copy of Bossuet's "Catechism," which Monsieur l'Abbé had procured for him by special favor, soon after the decree establishing this as the new catechism of the Gallican Church had been promulgated.

"I wish not to fail in my duty," the venerable priest explained, when the count had patiently listened to his scruples, "and my judgment belongs to another age. But the good God has made my judgment thus. And if Monsieur le Comte desires that this catechism be taught to the children of Val-Maria, might not Monsieur l'Abbé, who is more learned than I, better understand this duty?"

"Do not distrust yourself, dear father; let your conscience be your guide for all duty," the count answered, reverently. "I will talk the matter over with Monsieur l'Abbé, and meanwhile, will you lend me your copy?"

It was a pardonable subterfuge to free the

old man's tender conscience from the ceaseless perusal of the clauses that offended him, and he gave it to the count with a look of intense relief.

Montal had not yet given this catechism close study, though he knew, of course, of its promulgation, and a copy lay among other papers on his desk; but the good curé's strong feeling invested the subject with a new interest, and he turned over the pages of the pamphlet with a lively curiosity the moment he reached the château, being first attracted, as was natural, to a reading of some passages against which a wavering pencil-line was traced.

"*Question.* What are the duties of Christians towards their rulers; and what, in particular, are our duties towards Napoleon l., our Emperor?

"*Answer.* Christians owe to the princes who govern them, and we, in particular, owe to Napoleon l., our Emperor, love, respect, obedience, fidelity, military service, and the tributes ordained for the preservation and defence of the Empire and of his throne. To honor and serve the Emperor is, therefore, to honor and serve God.

"*Question.* Are there any special reasons which should more strongly attach us to our Emperor Napoleon I.?

"*Answer.* Yes; for it is he whom God raised up in difficult circumstances to restore the public profession of the holy religion of our forefathers, and to be its protector. He has restored public order by his profound and active wisdom; he defends the state by his powerful arm; and he has become the anointed of the Lord through the consecration of the Sovereign Pontiff, the head of the Universal Church.

"*Question.* What ought we to think of such persons as may fail in their duties towards our Emperor?

"*Answer.* According to the Apostle St. Paul they would therefore be resisting the orders of God Himself, and would become worthy of eternal damnation."

The document was indeed a curious one, and Montal could scarcely view it with unconcern when he remembered the unpleasant rumors that were gaining credence about the court, and the imperious purpose of the man thus deified—a purpose unassailable either by love or right.

But the next day's *Moniteur* seemed to reproach him for his lack of faith, with its glowing review of the interior growth and prosperity of the Empire, and its special indications in the imperial city. A triumphal arch was commenced at the Place du Carrousel, through which, on great occasions, the imperial cortége should be more fittingly received in the ancient palace that had hitherto been only the abode of kings. The beautiful column for the Place Vendôme, of which the model had been displayed early in the spring, was already begun,—a victor's column indeed, to be moulded from the cannon he had captured in battle, their deadly voices stilled into a running commentary of his praise, from base to capitol ; and how could it be otherwise when the conqueror himself kept guard over their speech, whether actually, in the tale they told, or silently, immovable as they?—an effigy in bronze scarcely sterner than the man it represented !

A plan for embanking the Seine with new quays had been adopted, and the work of demolition upon the neighborhood between the boulevards and the Tuileries had made considerable progress with a view to the embellishment of that entire portion of the city, in which ancient Paris would soon be no longer recognizable. One might read the names of the Napoleonic victories at the very street-corners, and seek, without disappointment, for the thread of each new drama, in some motif of that extraordinary life—the color being always eulogistic—as one might trace in permanant sculptured cornices, or ephemeral triumphant decorations, the glorified emblematic "*N*" embroidered with bees and fleur-de-lis.

The new stone bridge near the Jardin des Plantes bore the name of Austerlitz, appropriately enough, for the gardens were largely enriched with the spoils of Schönbrunn. The colonnade of the lordly building of the Louvre was nearly completed, its pediment had been given into the hands of a distinguished sculptor to receive its final decoration, and opposite this palace a wide and beautiful street, to be christened "Rivoli," was contemplated. Military schools were founded at Fontainebleau and Sainte-Cyr; and in the fields of art and science and literature every encouragement was devised by medals and pensions and princely orders for work. There was a new idea—whose might it be but his?—of an " Exhibit des Industries," in which the product of every existing species of industry should be represented for its further stimulus. Yet it was not so long since the clamoring people, scarcely better than a cowed mob, stood in the narrow streets crying for bread—bread, for which they paid extortionately with their scanty pence. The very streets they had darkened were beginning to disappear. Had the people and their grievance been utterly changed by the touch of this magic sceptre?

How could a grievance exist in the face of

such prosperity? or how might a doubting
heart excuse itself before such unexampled
proof?

But even while the atmosphere of this wonderful, smiling peace-activity seemed dominant, there was an undertone contradictory
and ominous. There was a vast military force
to be kept occupied, lest it should rise in rebellion, filling the lengthy hours of idleness
with schemes of dethronement too many humiliated princes were ready to lead—too many
discontents from other nations, stung by jeal-
ousy, were eager to enforce.

Hence ceaseless plans for new campaigns;
while with new triumphs grew the unappeas-
able desire to be everywhere victorious—by
land or sea; with a special, vindictive stirring up of English jealousies, and a constant
satirical, yet petty, agitation of differences
already sufficient. By the end of December,
1806, the conscription for 1807 had been
already levied; yet in April of 1807 Napoleon demanded from the Senate the levy for
1809.

If there was a party in France who watched for some outbreak of discontent at this unusual demand, it suffered in silence, for the pages of the faithful *Moniteur* continued to report the flattering addresses of the always obsequious Senate, calling attention to the Emperor's fatherly tenderness in guarding the inexperience of his children by thus summoning them so long before the legal levy, that they might be in training when required to march. Instead of any public protestations against the immense force that was being drained from the life of the nation to satisfy the ambitious projects of Napoleon, there were new and vehement assurances of gratitude.

Pierre still read out with unction to his little group in the square of Val-Maria such fragments of news as offered fitting texts for his homilies, retaining his large views for France, his pride in the army, and his patronizing approbation of the Emperor, although he had prudently abandoned his hopes of a duchy for the little Nanette, who had now grown into a rosy, brown-eyed maiden very pleasant to behold, and of an age to suggest the *dot* with which Pierre's thoughts had been recently occupied (failing the duchy), and which had already assumed very creditable proportions for a peasant bride. This pleasant state of things might have continued indefinitely, had it not been for an unexpected circumstance which one morning brought Yvonne in tears to the château to tell the countess that Pierre had drawn his " numéro" in the last conscription, "and there is only to go ; but Pierre is pale as death and speaks never a word, for you see, madame, he is very brave, my good Pierre ; he could march with the best ; but when one has handled flour for so long, the gun goes not so well ! and it takes courage to touch the *dot* of the little one, *mais enfin——"*

"Papa! papa!" Felix cried, imploringly, to the count, who was on the terrace with them.

"I understand, my boy," his father answered, smiling at his flushed and eager face. "You may help them if you wish, But you do not think it is the duty of Pierre to give loyal service to his Emperor?"

"I think Pierre will love him best if he stays!" the boy answered, impetuously. "I want no one to serve my Emperor, except for love!"

CHAPTER ELEVENTH.

HEN the count had returned to Val-Maria in the summer of 1806, after greeting his wife, his eyes had sought hers with troubled inquiry, for it was still early in the evening, and Felix was not waiting to welcome him.

"Dearest Louis, he is well and more beautiful than ever. Come and see," she had answered, reassuringly, as she led the way into her dressing-room and parted the curtain that fell between them and the chamber where their child lay sleeping. "He has never been so well; but he expends so much energy in the day that our dear Alfonte thinks he needs more sleep than other children."

She had paused on the threshold, speaking in low, cautioning tones. "I would not tell him you were coming, for he might not have slept all night, and he will be so happy in the morning! You cannot think what he is like when you only see him sleeping, for in the day he is so full of life—never for an instant still! You cannot look at him without knowing how happy he is ; a radiance seems to flash from him and make a halo about him—about everything where he passes. He is like a great, glowing ruby in our home!"

"She has lost herself completely in the joy of the child," her husband thought, in wonder at the new tones of gladness in her beloved voice, as she glided from him and stood, half hidden by the draperies of the little white couch, smiling down on their child with a face that was glorified by her passionate mother-love.

The room was flooded with moonlight, and in his sleep the child was indeed very beautiful —yet an ideal of motion at rest rather than of absolute rest—so instinct with life did he seem as he lay in his wonderful grace, the waves of

soft hair tossed back on his pillow stirring
softly in the odorous breeze that floated in at
the open window; the exquisite curves of the
face and limbs, touched with the soft rose-
flushes of sleep, seemed to throw off a shim-
mer of content with the rhythmic pulsations
of his breath. He was very child-like in his
sleep, only the brow and the large-lidded,
sleeping eyes with their long, dark fringes
were too noble for a little child, and as Montal
stood watching, the tumult of joy that had
come over him changed to a feeling of awe,
for it was like the brow of a seraph, he thought.
But as he looked, a holy calm grew upon him
and possessed him wholly, and he saw the
calm deepen on the rapt face of the mother,
which seemed fairer and rounder than when
he had seen it last, as she clasped her hands
and slowly drooped her head until it touched
the face of her boy, who, stirring in his
dream, half opened his eyes, with a smile, to
murmur, " *Madonna mia!*"

When at last they turned away, the count
made a motion to enter the studio, but she

held him back. " Felix must take you through the studio himself," she said; " for, Louis, you cannot think how wonderful his studies are ; even Alfonte calls them extraordinary !"

And so in truth the father thought them the next morning, as Felix, all animation, drew him with eager steps from one point to another, touching each cast with caressing fingers as he explained its meaning. It was always the same face—no one of them completed, but each sufficiently evolved to bring out the central thought.

"My boy, this brow is superb !" his father said, lingering before a study which revealed only the upper part of the head. "Why do you not finish your idea ?"

" Oh, it is all there," Felix answered, carelessly. " You see, papa, these are only *moods*. I learned that from the great Angelo when we were in Italy. I do not think that thought would change the lower part of the face: Signore Alfonte says so, too. Here he is planning for the good of France in the ' *Code Napoléon;*' but in *this* one"—drawing his father

swiftly across the room—" I had to model both
the mouth and eyes; for here he is grieving
over the soldiers he has lost in battle, and the
soldiers worship him. Do you think the
mouth would be like that? Signore Alfonte
has not seen this one yet."

"It is like the other—too fine not to be
finished," his father answered, in astonish-
ment that the boy could regard his work so
lightly.

" Oh, they are only studies for my master-
work," Felix explained, with charming simplicity. " When I want to keep an expression in my mind, I model it. I might forget
some of the ways he looks to me, for I am
always thinking about him. I want to *know*
the face in all its changes before I begin. Oh,
papa, do you see these copies of the little bust
you brought me from Paris? I have changed
them a little—I wanted to put another thought
in. Are they better, or not so good ?"

The youthful artist was flitting from side to
side of the great studio while he talked, with
motions as impetuous as his words, turning his

miniature casts to secure the best light for the expression he wished to emphasize.

"Felix, they are all wonderful. You have grown into an artist already; you will be a *great* artist some day. We must thank God."

His face was, if possible, more radiant than ever as he came back to his father's side. "I do, dear father, always. I am *very* happy. I have known for a long time that I should be a great artist: God told me so when I was very little."

"How did He tell you, my child?" his father questioned, reverently; the boy seemed like an inspiration—so beautiful and masterful—compelling belief in his strange moods.

"I cannot remember—it is so long ago; but you *have* to know a thing when God tells you. Michael Angelo always knew."

Felix stood in the midst of his models, turning his glowing glance from one to another, while a deep flush of content overspread his beautiful face. "I believe I know him *now* almost perfectly!" he exclaimed, with sudden conviction; "and the next time Signore Alfonte comes from Italy I shall be ready to block out my work. I believe I am ready *now !*" he cried, with the growing eagerness that was so characteristic, as he dwelt upon the idea. "It almost makes me tremble to wait."

Montal turned suddenly to hide the pain that the eager words awakened. It had seemed impossible not to be hopeful in this exuberant presence, and the association of his child's rare promise with the ripened genius and honored age of the great master, Angelo, had appeared like a natural and happy augury. The boy was so beautiful in his mood of inspiration that it was not strange to hear the young lips speak of "master-work;" and they were in truth wonderful, these "studies for the master-work," fashioned upon an ideal that had grown with the boy's life into a development that was nearly perfect, spiritually, intellectually, artistically—a conception that was possible only to a nature supremely endowed and exceptionally surrounded. But in some unaccountable way the young artist's soul seemed enthralled by the individuality of this man whom he had never seen ; even in the least-finished bits the identity of the face was unmistakable.

" I shall teach the people who do not know him to *love* my Emperor !" Felix cried, with an enthusiasm that filled his father's eyes with tears.

That evening, after Felix had left them, the count and countess strolled up and down the terrace together, far into the night, discussing the boy's marvellous gift, which had developed with almost inconceivable rapidity during the count's last long absence, and Montal seemed especially struck with the intense spirituality the always beautiful head had assumed under the boy's adoring touch.

" What shall we do?" the countess asked, with a sigh, " since he means it for a portrait. Yet his illusions are so beautiful, and he is so happy in them !"

"Shall we dispel his illusions, sweet mother, or he ours? Must we not hold such genius sacred ?" Montal answered, reverently. " The child is nearer heaven than we."

The beautiful faith touched and tranquillized

him, and was essentially helpful in overcoming
the cynicism towards which his mental rest-
lessness was tending. For perhaps the child,
whose eyes were too pure to behold iniquity,
had a lesson for his world-saddened heart, he
told himself, yearningly ; for he still longed,
with the eagerness of youth, to believe in the
nobility of one who might have been so great.

For several winters, during the sessions of
the Senate, the countess had passed some
months in her old Florentine home, that Felix
might have every advantage for the study of
his art, in which, boy as he was, he had already
become absorbed. From thence they had gone
to Rome ; and in every art-gallery and studio,
in the churches and public squares, the gentle,
courteous, white-haired master and the beautiful boy—the brother artists—were familiar fig-
ures. But Rome had not the permanent charm
for the little artist that Florence possessed.

He had astonished his mother by his reply
to her question as to why he was so anxious
to leave Rome for Florence.

"It is beautiful to see the Holy City once ;

but I think I have not time for Rome, *Madonna mia;* for God has told me that I must be an artist."

"But, my darling, Rome is full of art-treasures—full of the work of your great master, Angelo. You must come here to study him at his best."

"I love to stand under the grand duomo," the boy responded, musingly, "because he planned it. And the 'Moses' is so sublime that it makes me tremble. But I do not want to stay in Rome always, because—because I think in Rome they only care for the religion of the Pope ; they do not love my art, as they do in Florence."

"Is not the religion of the Pope *our* religion?" the countess asked, hurt and startled.

"I used to think so, *Madonna mia,* when we were always in Val-Maria, and Monsieur le Curé told me about the Holy Father. But *now* I do not feel it so. I think often of Monsieur le Curé : it is good for him not to be in Rome. He would not love the Church so much if he were here."

m

" You are only a child, my Felix," his mother answered, in a voice full of tender reproof, " or you would know that we may not speak so of our Holy Church."

Felix threw his arms caressingly about his mother, full of self-chiding for the pain in her face and tone.

" If I could tell you what I mean, *Madonna mia carissima !*" he cried, imploringly, and filling the soft Italian syllables with a wealth of love and reverence, " you would not think me wrong. I want to go away to love it more. These great festivals at St. Peter's make me afraid. God seems so far away—on Easter Day I could not think of Him at all, it was all so magnificent to see, like the court of a Roman emperor. I do not think Monsieur le Curé would be happy here."

She did not know what to answer him, and Alfonte, who had been listening in silent amazement, returned to a thought which had also seemed strange to him.

" Felix, why do you say they love our art less in Rome than in Florence ?"

" You have the same reason, dear master," the boy answered, brightly.

" Ah, well, it has passed from me unconsciously, then, into the keeping of my pupil," Alfonte returned, entering at once into his playful humor. " And I must ask it of him again."

Felix was instantly grave.

"I feel it so much, I cannot make you understand," he said, after a moment's pause of hesitation, but his words were as impetuous as ever. " It is more beautiful here, but I think art has come to Rome to *make* it beautiful; and in Florence it *had* to be there, because the air was full of it: it was *born* there."

"I have spoiled you with my tales of Lorenzo dei Medici, and our dreamings over the gardens of San Marco, with its wonderful art-treasures," Alfonte confessed, laughing. " But it was a fairy tale fit for the food of an artist," he continued, the enthusiasm which had naturally infected Felix returning at the mere mention of these days of the greatness of

Florence, "and if the school of that beautiful past were still there, I myself would obtain admission for you like a modern Granacci, and perhaps we should see another Angelo, though I think we should not have a subject half-pagan for our first work, like the faun in the Uffizzi.

"But what a part for a prince to act!" Alfonte cried, warming into the tale of which Felix never wearied, of the boyhood of Michael Angelo, of Lorenzo's munificence, his judgment, his keen interest in youthful talent, his wise discoveries that seemed akin to predictions of genius, the judicious criticism and stimulus and attrition of the brilliant circle into which he introduced his youthful aspirants for art, teaching them to know and to strive for excellence. "Ah, truly, for this it were worth being a prince!"

"If an artist were not better, dear master," said Felix, softly, coming very close to him, and looking up with happy, luminous eyes.

"Dear countess," said Alfonte then quite pleadingly, for he thought she still looked sad at the confession of Felix, "can you not pardon

your two capricious artists if they sigh, even
here, for the Loggia and the Gates of Paradise?"

*   *   *   *   *   *   *   *   *   *

After the count's withdrawal from political
life, it had cost him a great effort to abandon
the hope of still doing something for the
France he loved; but as the months passed,
rumors of discontent were rising—there was
more than one attempt at assassination; the
current of court-life grew no clearer, and when
Josephine finally retired heart-broken to Malmaison, and the Senate theatrically proclaimed
that their Emperor had given to his people the
last and costliest proof of sacrifice, Montal
turned so bitter in his heart against the man
he had once striven to uphold, that he felt
there was no safety for him so long as he occupied himself with thoughts of the France of
the present.

At first there was a blank, in which he
seemed capable of nothing except the fierce
resolution to keep himself from following
events as they were daily chronicled. The
peals of rejoicing that sounded so soon along

the route from Vienna to Paris penetrated even
the depths of his quiet study at Val-Maria, and
were almost maddening to him ; for it was
not an easy matter for this statesman who had
striven so faithfully to serve his country, to go
back, with a headlong plunge, to the old literary interests of early days.   But the wonderful journals of his grandfather, inwrought
with so much that was dear in his childhood,
brought back these memories, his conscience
helped him, and the calm, beautiful, loving
atmosphere of his home-life made it possible
for him at last.

And then came beautiful days, when he had
struggled up into an ideal world of aspiration
and of art, where the frettings of the tempest
out of which he had been tossed scarcely
reached him; he found it again possible to
realize a living companionship in the great
minds of the past, and to find comfort in the
greatness of those who had lived for noble ends.

The beautiful child had developed into a tall,
slender youth, with a face and bearing remind-
ing one of Raphael's portrait as given us by

the Sanzio himself—a resemblance that was possibly increased by his usual dress of dark-green velvet, fashioned like the tunic of Raphael which had pleased the young artist's fancy. His soft, bright hair curled loosely about his throat, in a mode that was usual with young noblemen of those days, but it had a peculiar richness, as if light were always playing through it, ready at any moment to touch the brown waves with the red-gold tints that artists love. His brow was very sweet and serious, almost contradicting the spirit of the dark, luminous eyes, which were radiant with an intense glow of love and joy that was almost unearthly. The bounding, exuberant life of his childhood seemed gradually etherealizing into a spirituality which ruled those about him resistlessly while under the spell of his presence.

Thus the days seemed flooded with sunshine for mother and son, as they worked and talked in the great studio of the Château of Val-Maria. Often the master was with them, for he could no longer be parted from Felix, and now he made but short journeys to his old home, seeming only to live fully when in the boy's presence; frequently the count left his books and joined them there; sometimes the old curé was with them; but Felix was always the centre of the group, his slim, tapering fingers trembling with artistic instinct, eagerly working out his last new thought, while, in his unsconscious, masterful way, giving the keynote to the talk which rippled with life, gladness, and love over an ever-implied, yet rarely spoken, thought of God and art which made it a ceaseless song of praise.

Such was his spell.

Only in the wakeful hours that would come to her at night did the mother remember that he had seemed slighter, more easily fatigued; but in the morning his smile would compel hers again, while the spell of his radiance overcame her anxiety.

"There is nothing to make you sad, *Madonna mia*," he said, one morning, as she raised the portière of his studio and confronted him suddenly, before the shadow of the night's grieving had left her face. "God is so good, and life is so beautiful, and love is so sweet!"

"Yes, my treasure," she answered, clinging to him with an uncontrollable yearning, "life is beautiful, and love is sweet—oh, *very* sweet!"

He passed his arm around her and drew her head very tenderly to his shoulder—for he was already taller than she—and standing so for a moment, he smiled down upon her silently with a great love that calmed and comforted her, until the light of the wonderful joy in his smile drew her again under the spell that made the sunshine of her days.

"You are too sad, sweet mother," he said, still charming her with his eyes, full of a great, tender, understanding love, "so I have made this for you, with a face I should love you to wear—for life is very beautiful."

She started and shrank as he drew the cover from a little marble bust he had placed upon her table : it was her own face that she recognized, but radiant as if she had never known a sorrow.

"Oh, Felix!" she cried, almost with involuntary reproof, "my darling, you do not know! I shall never look like that."

He clasped her closer, looking at her steadily with that wonderful, growing light in his eyes.

"*Madonna mia,*" he said, in a low voice full of assurance, "you *will* look like that some day. God has shown you to me in my dreams, and I have made this portrait for you: it is so beautiful to be glad!"

"Dear Felix, we cannot always be glad."

"I wish I could show you my dreams, sweet mother; they comfort me."

"They comfort you, Felix? Why do you need comfort? Do you suffer?" she questioned, in quick alarm.

"Only because you are sad sometimes," he answered, very tenderly. "But God is good, and life and love have no end; you will grow to look like my dream—some day."

CHAPTER TWELFTH.

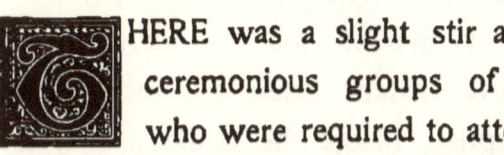HERE was a slight stir among the ceremonious groups of courtiers who were required to attend in the Emperor's apartments at the Tuileries at the hour of his earliest levée, as a cavalier in his riding-dress, which showed the disorder of haste, passed quickly from chamber to chamber, unannounced, his only passport being the words "extreme urgency," which he repeated from door to door, with a face whose look of tortured strength could not be gainsaid. He had ridden all night, fresh horses awaiting him at each post, and the courier who had been sent before to crave an audience had ridden not so fast as he.

Monsieur de Talleyrand was just leaving the Emperor's private study as the Count of Montal reached it, and the punctilious, unemotional minister received his old acquaintance with a glance of unfeigned disapproval, as, scarcely pausing for recognition, he passed unannounced into the imperial presence.

He had the air of a courier fresh from a battle-field, with news of grave import, and the Emperor, always on the alert, turned to him with instant attention, recognizing, to his surprise, before he could speak, the senator who had formerly done him good service, but who had not for years appeared at court.

"Sire!" Montal cried to the astonished monarch, without preamble or apology, "My only child lies dying! Out of his passionate love for you he has wrought a great work for France. He asks to deliver it into your hands."

For the day had come when the great work was finished, and the Château of Val-Maria was again filled with guests. Alfonte, the master, had been summoned from Italy, and he stood, bowed with emotion, before his pupil's marvellous achievement. "It is wonderful!" he answered to the mother's questioning eyes, "and I know not if the angels or the spirit of the great Angelo himself has taught him, for he has a white, white soul!"

And then, in a voice that struggled to be calm, he pleaded to be left alone with the lesson of this great creation.

"My God, my God!" he prayed, in uncontrollable anguish, "how inscrutable are Thy ways! If but my gray hairs and my life full of years might be given for the life of the boy! If my death might but save his genius to the world! And oh, my God! I thought myself his master—forgive the presumption. Yet it was Thy will; for had I not been blind, I had not dared to teach his little artist feet to stand. I was not worthy of the honor, and Thy ways are past finding out. But, oh, my Father, it would be sweet to give my life for the life of the child!"

Later the good old curé came and stood

spell-bound before the image, unconsciously removing the close-fitting black cap that crowned his flowing locks, as if in a majestic presence. "The boy knows no evil," he said. "My God, I thank thee! So are our hearts at peace, for heaven must soon be his home. Yet I knew not that the good God permitted men to be so godlike! If our Emperor is thus, let him have all power!"

The court physician, an early friend of Montal, who had known Felix from his birth, had arrived with his suite and occupied one of the wings of the château. And the other wing contained the chapel which the effigies and tombs of the knights of Montal and the gifts of a long line of devoted ancestry had enriched and filled with historic charm; and here Monseigneur the Archbishop of Paris had deigned to pass the night, that he might offer the Church's consolation with fullest honors to a daughter so faithful and self-sacrificing as the countess had proved herself in caring for the Church's interests.

These two great men who knew the Em-

peror so intimately had crossed the threshold
of the studio together and stood before the
statue in amazement, avoiding each other's
gaze, as its full, sublime meaning grew upon
them. The archbishop crossed himself, but
spoke no word, as he passed into the chamber
where the countess sat, with bright, strained
eyes and heightened color, watching her boy;
but when he had lingered over him in silent
and awe-struck blessing, he reverently kissed
the mother's hands that were folded each upon
each, as if in a convulsive prayer for calm, with
a touch so sympathetic that they lay together
more lightly.

Another guest was coming, more mighty
than they—unbidden, invisible; yet, in his
approach, subduing that household with the
majesty that none may resist. Only in the
eyes of the boy the smile brightened and inten-
sified with a beauty they could scarcely bear to
look upon. The faces of those that loved him
had turned away from his as Felix sought them,
and the faithful abbé had knelt beside the
couch and buried his face in the pillows. Only

the mother grew strong for the need of the moment, and smiled back at her darling with a look of unutterable love, that she might not seem to fail in sharing this last joy of his life, as she realized the meaning of the sounds from without that had reached his eager ears.

"He comes," he said, simply. "1 know his step !"

A moment before the imperial travelling-carriage had dashed through the little square that led to the bridge : the evening bells were sounding for vespers, with a rustic chime that recalled the bells of the little church at Rueil where Josephine lay buried. Always, in the olden days, Napoleon had paused to listen as those bells rang out, and now the chime cleared like magic the brow knitted with complicated schemes for the subjugation of Austria, for the humiliation of England, for the reconciliation of Murat—schemes which were maturing to his unprecedented satisfaction in the solitude and rapid motion of the journey.

It calmed for an instant that bitter longing

for a word from Marie Louise—for news of the boy for whom he had sacrificed his honor as a man—his pledge of all that was sacred—the happiness, nay, perhaps the *life* of the wife he had once truly loved.

Across the fierce conflicts, the dangers, the triumphs, the machinations of these Hundred Days which should be forever memorable in the annals of the world, the sound swept like a cool, beneficent wave obliterating the feverish consciousness of the *now*, bearing him back into the past, and enveloping him with the charm of those early days at Saint-Cloud.

As in those days it had been his wont, he yielded himself wholly, for the moment, to the spell of those rustic church-bells, and in an instant the rushing horses had been checked by his imperious signal, and he alighted from the carriage and stood, with bowed head, listening till the chime had ceased.

The shrine of the Madonna Val-Maria was dimly illuminated with sputtering candles which still further defaced its ugliness, as they burned with a sickly glare in the beautiful rich light of the sunset, with slow, ceaseless drippings down the blackened stone. And before it knelt a peasant woman so absorbed in grief and prayer that she was unconscious of any disturbing presence, as the hot tears dropped on the toil-worn hands in which the crucifix was so tightly clasped that its image left its impress on their rough surfaces. A strong, true, loving face was visible under the white coiffe, and from her simple and beautiful heart had come the votive offering so inconsonant with the strength and purity of her emotion, and which, in this supreme moment, failed to give her any comfort; though never before— even when her own little Jean had died—had she brought half this number to the shrine of the Madonna Val-Maria.

"Oh, Holy Mother!" she prayed, with streaming tears, "thou knowest the grief will kill our sweet lady! And Monsieur Felix! —he is an angel to the people. Oh, Madonna Val-Maria, have mercy!"

" Is there one now living who could weep so for me?" the great Emperor questioned in his softened heart, as he entered his carriage again without attracting the suppliant's notice, and was borne swiftly on to the interview for which Felix so eagerly waited.

As the door of the sick-chamber opened to admit him, the boy raised himself on his couch with feverish strength, stretching out both hands, and turning towards him a face transfigured by indescribable emotion. "Sire!" he cried, in a voice that rang like an electric thrill through the group, "how holy it is to have power over the joy of the world !"

And after a moment's pause to rally strength, the words came slowly and unsteadily, with a pathetic intensity—

" I leave you—the message of my life—for France: my love for my Emperor——"

There was an irresistible gesture of command in the frail, extended hand, and unconsciously the Emperor moved forward. The heavy folds of the velvet curtain which had been placed in Felix's hand, in answer to his mute appeal, swung aside from the boy's failing grasp as the Emperor reached it, the bullion fringes sweeping the floor like the muffled crash of artillery, and the Man of Destiny stood face to face—and alone—with the boy's masterful work of love.

It was like a chapel for stillness: the litter of the workshop all removed; the rude outlines hidden under the deep crimson hangings that swept from skylight to floor; only on the left the lower casements were open, and the western light flooded the marble that rose majestic and beautiful before him, wrought with the passion of the pure young life.

It was of heroic size and mysteriously beautiful—the conception of an intense love, spiritualized by the boy's holy dreams.

The perfect outlines of the face the world knows well had been preserved : the brow, noble with an intellect never surpassed, here showed a further grandeur, almost as of a divine prescience ; the mouth, beautiful and sweet and stern, wore the added grace of love; all the noble and poetic possibilities of his nature had been sought out and carried to their loftiest height; everything that was ignoble had been purged away. It was as if once, in awe of his own great gifts and power, the man had communed with himself and with God in solemn consecration, praying, "Conform me to Thine image!"

It was the face of the man with the soul of an angel.

He was alone in the stillness, with the glory of the tribute, and the conqueror's eyes gleamed with triumph. Should the world indeed know him thus—so magnificent—so godlike?

The intoxication of past triumphs floated like incense about him; the shouts of adoring multitudes caressed him with his greatness; yet even this one more added proof was sweet —naming him Cæsar—Invincible!

But suddenly these pageants faded as the light sank in the west; the flush paled on the beautiful marble image, and the white, love-wrought message of the statue chilled him to the soul.

The lost opportunities of his life thronged about him, stifling the air with their presence and voices :

An all-embracing intellect divorced from the rule of right.

Great gifts perverted ; the mastery of men's hearts—used to crush them ; the comprehension of men's characters—used to dwarf them.

Holy rights violated; sacred influences disregarded; the voices of overturned princes calling to him from the steps of desolated thrones; the voices of hapless men and women calling to him from the downward paths he had made it easy for them to tread.

The wail of exiles who had thwarted his will reached him across the distance ; the death-groans of thousands who died for love of him came back from silenced battle-plains ; and above them all the voice of the murdered D'Enghien saying, "He is noble ; plead my cause before him ;" the voice of Josephine, full of prayers and tears——

And through this havoc of greatness, pitiless and cold as hail, stormed the memory of his own words, uttered as a creed, *" I am not an ordinary man, and the laws of morals and of customs were never made for me !"*

And out of the shadows that deepened around him did some near vision of the future loom ? Did he see the young Empress, standing on the ashes of her broken faith, recreant to France, deaf to his imploring words, bartering her freedom for an Italian duchy ? Did he see the English, lashed to fury by his jealous pride, wreaking their vengeance in his betrayal? Did he see his own little child, a prisoner in the imperial palace of Schönbrunn, with yearning, unhappy eyes and outstretched arms, calling to him in tones that sobbed like the rise and fall of waves against the relentless rocks of St. Helena ?

* * * * * * * * * *

The unwelcome guest—the invincible monarch—had entered that hushed chamber as the curtain fell behind the Emperor, and on the couch Felix lay—peaceful, smiling, still—his little life rounded in the knowledge of perpetual love, his fair spirit crowned with the unfading strength God holds in store for those who love the Beauty of Holiness.

THE END,